# Molly's Cue

# Molly's Cue

## ALISON ACHESON

www.coteaubooks.com

Edited by Laura Peetoom

**Library and Archives Canada Cataloguing in Publication**

Acheson, Alison, 1964–
    Molly's cue / Alison Acheson.

ISBN 978-1-55050-430-9

    I. Title.

PS8551.C32M64 2010      jC813'.54      C2010-901018-3

2517 Victoria Avenue
Regina, Saskatchewan
Canada    S4P 0T2
www.coteaubooks.com

*Available in Canada from:*
Publishers Group Canada
9050 Shaughnessy Street
Vancouver, British Columbia
Canada    V6P 6E5

*Available in the US from:*
Orca Book Publishers
www.orcabook.com
1-800-210-5277

10  9  8  7  6  5  4  3  2  1

Coteau Books gratefully acknowledges the financial support of its publishing program by: the Saskatchewan Arts Board, the Canada Council for the Arts, the Government of Canada through the Canada Book Fund, the Government of Saskatchewan through the Creative Economy Entrepreneurial Fund, the Association for the Export of Canadian Books and the City of Regina Arts Commission.

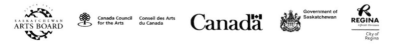

*For Amy –*
*for her wisdom and laughter.*

# Exit Grand

*P*eople who knew my grandmother – we called her Grand – always said she was something else.

*And she was. She wasn't like anyone I knew.*

*Uncle Early said she was first in line when make-believe was handed out.*

*Mom said she was in an orbit all her own: she was the star and we were the planets. I remember when she said that. She turned red immediately and looked rather angry with herself for saying such a thing aloud. At the time, Early chuckled. And when Grand died last April, he said Grand was now in her own obit…but that's Early for you. I told him to be more respectful, but maybe another bad pun was his way of grieving. Everyone has their own way, Mom says. Though it's hard to know just what Mom's is.*

*Sometimes it doesn't seem possible that Grand's gone. When she was with us she made me want to feel the stage beneath my feet and the spotlight on my face. Grand belonged to the stage, and the stage belonged to Grand. I could always feel her with me — in some way — on stage. She said it belonged to me, too, to both of us together. She always said that, and I believed her. Because Grand knew everything. At least, everything that was important.*

# 1
# Finally

*H*igh school. Finally!" There are kids all around us. "It won't take long," I tell Candace, "and we'll know where everything is." She doesn't look convinced. I remind her: "Art class."

Her face clears. "Right. Art class. And you — drama. And Ms. Tanaka."

Three years ago Ms. Tanaka moved from New York City to our blip on the map. Why, I don't want to question. I've been waiting to be in her class, to step onto a stage that is more than a platform at the end of a stinky gym. For me, that's what high school is going to be about.

But standing in this wide entrance hallway, brightly coloured banners overhead swaying with all the movement below, I suddenly wonder. Candace's face has taken on a pinched look. And there's something in me that feels pretty much as she looks, and it's something I've never felt before.

Maybe it's the sheer size of the place. Landing Middle School had three hundred students. This place has more than five times that. And right now, every one of them is running around us.

"It's not going to be that different, though," I tell Candace. "Really."

"How do we find anything?" is all she says, and seconds later a tall guy in a red cap jostles her, and the stuff in her arms flies everywhere.

"Hey!" I call out. He keeps going. "Hey!" I shout. "What's up with you, Red Cap?" He seems to pause then, but Candace is pulling on my sleeve.

"Don't yell," she says. "Help me pick up my stuff." Even as she speaks, I can hear a boot connect with her pencil case, and it spins across the floor.

"What sort of place is this? Where people just knock each other down?" My voice rises, and it feels good, as if the loudness might push down this new queasy feeling.

Candace stops trying to put her binders together and looks at me. "What's the matter with you, Molly Gumley? Why are you yelling?"

"Nothing's the matter. And don't call me Molly...you know." If there's one thing I really don't like about myself, it's my last name.

I scrooch down to help her pick up the rest of her stuff — her lunch bag and that pencil case she's had in her desk for as long as I've known her. There's a huge dusty footprint across the faded polka-dot cotton. A hand picks up the case and hands it to me, and I look up to see a flash of red and an apologetic smile. "Sorry about this," Red Cap says. His eyes are gold-brown. I didn't know eyes could be that colour. I don't like how I can't come up with any words, so I pass the case to Candace as he turns away, and I can see that she hasn't noticed The Eyes. She reaches for the case. "This was one of Mom's projects for her first kids' sewing-crafts book."

"Come on," I say, and ignore the sad tone that keeps popping up lately when she talks about her mom. "Let's find the class lists." I find hers first. "Ozols, Candace," I read. "Mr Pritchard, room 208, and now for the G list." I head to the other wall where there's a huge sheet of paper posted with the letter G on top. Then I see…Ms. Tanaka. Candace sees her at the same moment.

"There she is," she whispers. "Looking just like she does in the newspaper!"

There have been articles about her in the local newspaper. Once they even had pictures of all her family. Every member of Ms. Tanaka's family has been on stage. Even her great-grandparents. They were vaudevillians. Thanks to Grand, I know all about vaudeville. "Go say hello!" Candace pushes me gently. And that feeling starts up again.

I'm going to ignore it, I decide, and I march over to the drama teacher. "I'm Molly," I say, and fight an urge to curtsey.

That would be too weird. Ms. Tanaka takes my hand and pumps it in a firm handshake. "Molly Gumley!" she says. "Coming from Landing Middle. You're in my Grade 9 drama class."

"You know me?" Jittery stuff sputters in my voice, I'm sure.

Ms. Tanaka has an amazing laugh: her jaw drops, and the sound comes from the back of her rib cage. "This must seem like a big school to you, but it's a small community. I'm a friend of Mr. Roman's. He mentioned you did a fine job as Dorothy."

Mr. Roman, my Grade 8 teacher. "Did he tell you I made Toto throw up?"

I didn't have to say that, did I? But it's worth it for her laugh.

"He did mention something about a few cookies. I'm rather fond of chocolate myself. He also said you were one of the most promising students he's ever had."

She gives me this sharp look, as if she's trying to see why he would have said that. Why wouldn't he? I want to say. But it's her unspoken question that hangs in the air.

Ms. Tanaka glances at her watch. "You should be finding your homeroom now." The bell cuts off her words and, with one final x-ray look, she's off and the hallway clears until it's just me and that question.

We belong to the stage, Grand always said. *Everyone* said — it's a family thing. I've never had somebody look at me with a question in their eyes. Not this question anyway, a "what's in you" question. I've never felt this…what is it that I feel?

Then the thought hits: this is it! This is the High School Thing that people talk about. When people ask, "So how do you feel about high school?" this is what they're talking about.

How have I been answering this past half a year? "I can't wait," is what I've been saying, and I'll stick to that. That's my plan. Here I am. It's where I've wanted to be. Except, I'm still in the hall and not in the classroom where I'm supposed to be.

## 2
# It's Going to be Easy

**I** find Candace in the cafeteria. She has her lunch laid out in front of her, and she's staring at it. I plop mine on the table. "How was art class?"

She rearranges the plums and a stack of crackers. "It's not what I was hoping it would be," she says, and looks up, her eyes filling with sudden tears.

I bite into my sandwich, unsure what to say.

She's blinking furiously. "I think most people in the class are there because they think it's going to be easy." She fiddles with the crackers again, and fans them out around a plum. "And Mr. Kerrigan, the teacher, I don't think he knows…anything!" Her voice wails in a way I've never heard before, and she claps a hand over her mouth, looking as surprised as I must.

Then Red Cap sits down beside me.

"Cool," he says, and reaches across the table towards

Candace. "Do you mind?" He places a grape at each outside corner of a cracker.

Candace sniffs loudly like a kindergarten kid, and reaches for her knapsack in a motion that has become familiar this past summer, ever since her grandpa gave her his old carving knife and taught her how to use it. She carries it on her, along with a piece of wood. It's become a thing she does when she's anxious. Lately, that's often.

"That's not what I think it is, is it?" hisses Red Cap, just as her hand appears with the knife over the tabletop. In one motion, he's moved to her side of the table and he's pushed her hand back into the sack. "Are you crazy?" He nods off to the corner of the cafeteria where a woman stands stiffly at attention, wearing a navy golf shirt marked LUNCH MON-ITOR. Her face is narrow and has a locked-in expression. "She takes her job *seriously*," he whispers.

Another sniff from Candace. More blinking.

"You can't bring that here," goes on Red Cap. He pats her hand as she pulls it away, minus the knife, and then he does up the zipper on the knapsack as if she really is a little kid.

"It's just for carving," she hisses right back at him. "Whittling."

"I know," he says. "I saw the piece of wood. But just the same — you can't bring it here. You'll have to look for some other artistic outlet." His funny choice of words and the irresistable grin that comes with them are completely lost on Candace. But not on me.

She's not going to let go of her misery so easily. "There's nothing artistic about this place!" she mutters.

"An artist can find it anywhere," he says, and his voice still has a teasing tone. It's hard to know if he's serious.

He gets up to leave and I move over, wondering if he just might return to his earlier seat, but no, he's off. Not without a wink first though. "Take care of her," he says to me. "This is a big place." As he walks away, I see another boy – looks like someone from our homeroom, I think – who shadows him.

I don't realize that I'm staring after him until I turn back to Candace and she looks sort of red. I wish, for a second, that he could see how angry she is.

"Do you think that, too? That I should be able to find art anywhere? Even in this place, with teachers like Mr. Kerrigan?" She begins to stuff her lunch back into the fabric sack she always carries it in. Back at Landing Middle School we weren't allowed any disposables in our lunches, and I see the habit has continued with Candace.

"I don't know," I say, and regret it instantly.

"You don't know? Well, you should know... something!"

I don't point out to her that she's not making much sense right now. She's busy trying to make that poor sack into the smallest possible object, rolling it in her hands, tighter and tighter.

And I'm a bit stumped as to what to say to her. "Are you getting your period?" I ask finally.

Candace waves her hands at me as if shooing me away. "No! It's nothing like that! Is that all you can come up with?"

I begin to eat my lunch. There's nothing else I can do. Others are finishing theirs. The garbage cans are filling; the tables have trays with Styrofoam and plastic utensils, cans, and juice boxes.

Candace gives a sort of shudder, and next thing I know, she's up and picking at all that stuff – that garbage. What's she thinking? "Help me," she says.

"Help you what?"

"Take it out to the hall."

Instead, I watch as she does. At first, only one or two people notice her, and they shake their heads and leave. It is, after all, the first day of school and after lunch it's over except for picking up books and handing forms in to the office and hanging out. Of course, Candace, being Candace, doesn't notice them shaking their heads. Stuff like that doesn't matter to her.

I go to the doorway and watch from there. She's forming the letter R with soda cans. Then E with lunch bags and wrappings. Then C with juice boxes. I can see what's coming. And every time she passes me in the doorway, she casts me the angriest look. I finally begin to help her round up the last of the cans. A few other kids are helping, too, by then.

The RECYCLE collage fills the entrance hall, and kids are gathered in a wide circle when Mr. Anderson, the principal, comes in. With him is Ms. Weir, the VP.

"What's the gathering...?" he starts to say, then stops when he sees Candace's work.

He pauses. Candace doesn't even notice him, she's so intent on her work with the final E.

I realize there's a silence in the hall. It's only momentary — no one wants to seem to be waiting for Mr. Anderson's response. But it is there — the waiting silence. Along with elbow nudges and eyebrow rising. Mr. Anderson walks the length of the work, and finally Candace notices him. The anxiety on her face is smoothed somewhat. Must be all the work with her hands that's done that.

She doesn't say anything, just waits.

Mr. Anderson clears his throat. "What do you think, Ms. Weir? It's an effective reminder. Raise a little cafeteria consciousness."

"I concur, Mr. A," says the VP.

"I concur, too," comes a voice. The voice I've been hearing all day.

The principal looks at him. "You must be Russell's brother. You look like twins."

Red Cap grins. "I'm Julian."

"Well, Julian," the principal says, "who is our artist?"

Candace speaks up. "Candace Ozols."

Mr. Anderson motions to the enormous bulletin board on the wall, almost empty except for a few handbills about summer programs. "Perhaps you can relocate it so that it won't be destroyed by 9:05 tomorrow. It will be a fine exhibit for Blue Point High, yes!"

At the word 'exhibit,' Candace breaks into a grin. Behind the principal's back, Red Cap wags an I-told-you-so finger.

Mr. Anderson goes into his office across the hall and opens the blinds that cover the window to the hallway. He gives a thumbs-up.

"Find art, make art," says Julian with a grin. "And we'll help." He looks at me. "Right?"

"Right," I say with a twinge of guilt over not helping earlier. My turn, for my art, will come tomorrow. Ms. Tanaka. Drama class.

## 3

# Chosen One

One face is familiar in drama class. Julian. "Thought I was too old for Grade 9, huh?" He doesn't lower his voice. "I did a grade over when I was a kid. Which means one thing now: I'm gonna drive before any of you!"

A girl speaks up. "Good. You can be our chauffeur." Her hair looks like a stubbly fall wheat field. Julian puts a hand to the girl's head. Not a hair moves. I reach out, too, and she doesn't pull away. Her hair feels exactly as it looks. "If you're gonna touch me, you'd better know my name," she says. "Katherine."

"And I'm Julian. Julian Smart."

*An actor's name.*

"I'm Molly," I say. *You ever heard of an actress named Gumley? Nope.*

Ms. Tanaka enters the room, with a sheaf of posters over

her arm. She begins to affix them to the giant bulletin board. One is for Dogwood Players Camp, a summer camp. "Start saving your money so you can go next summer," she says.

I've been saving for over a year now. I've only ever been to the little kids' camp that Grand paid for when I was in primary. Dogwood is the best, I've heard.

"We have a busy year ahead," Ms. Tanaka continues. "In a week I want you to present a monologue or dialogue to the class. The following week we are going to hold auditions for..." she pauses, "*The Sound Of Music*, our November performance. And that Monday, I'll draw ten names for the variety show that our school has every December. If you'd like to have your name in the jar, please fill out one of these." She waves a handful of blue papers. Almost everyone reaches for one. Amidst the voices, she goes on to explain some of what we're going to do: words like improvisation and interaction, projection and memorization. And she hands out books.

Katherine grabs a book of "Dialogues for Teens," and waves at me. "Want to work with me, Molly?"

I nod as Julian pops into view. "Gonna leave me out?" he says.

Katherine sticks out her tongue and laughs. "You're on your own," she says, and he pretends to pout.

I wish he could know what I'm thinking: *That's Katherine speaking, not me.*

But it's all fun for Julian. I'm beginning to get the feeling he doesn't take anything too seriously. He walks away with a grin, off to find his own project.

Almost time for the bell to ring and Ms. Tanaka says, "Just one more thing I'd like to do today." She leads the way out the door and down a short hallway to a plain single door. "I trust you're familiar with the front of the theatre, but today I'd like to show you backstage."

This must be the door. Inside my long sleeves, my arms feel prickly and I shiver. I think of all the times Grand brought me to performances, and the annual dance recitals that I've taken part in here, but still...this is different. Now it's me, as an actor, backstage. Ms. Tanaka's eyes focus on me, and she nods. "Go ahead."

Julian speaks, softly. "You're the chosen one."

I ignore him and turn the door handle. Inside it's dark and Ms. Tanaka touches a light switch, but it's a single bulb, quite high.

Front of house lights shine dimly through red velvet curtains, and a breeze moves the heavy fabric in gentle rhythmic waves that make me think of a beating heart. Pulleys hang from the ceiling. Yes. Arteries. Veins. Grey back curtains. Lungs. Here are the guts of the thing – that's how it feels. Something inside me goes silent.

I felt that silence once before – on a windy Sunday morning – unlike anything I'd experienced. I remember staring up into the branches of a grandly enormous cottonwood. I think it was Uncle Early – who else – who told me that cottonwoods are shallow rooted, and it doesn't take much to knock them down. Any bit of wind will do. I remember looking up, up into that old tree and, though it moved in a most frightening way, I stayed where I was. There was something magical about the wind and that tree. As there is here, in the shadows of backstage.

Classmates move in and out of dressing rooms and then they clatter off towards the stairs at the front of the stage. The bell rings. From far away rooms, and pouring into hallways, there are the sounds of hundreds of feet and voices.

"Molly?" It's Ms. Tanaka.

"I'm coming." I don't move.

Her voice is soft. "You can let yourself out." The door clicks behind her.

I walk through the pulleys, the bits of back curtain, step around old set pieces, feel the velvet curtains brush my face as I step upstage. There are rows of seats illuminated in exit lights. What is it to hear laughter from them? Pin-drop silence? Applause?

The cottonwood had stood firm. I'd been given that moment to stand there and look up into it, safe, even as it swayed and lurched. I've been lucky: I've seen magic; I've had Grand; I have what I want in my veins.

So why do I feel a gust of wind?

# 4

# Freedom and Dreams

The walk home is ten minutes. Candace turns right onto her street, the one before mine. A few more steps and I can see my front porch, and Early's old VW Bug in the driveway, bright orange and shouting spray-painted words. FREEDOM across the back. The paint looks still wet. PEACE is fading, but still discernible. Mom says he'll never grow up. She says it with a tone of frustration and, I think, a little envy. I like my uncle just as he is. I break into a jog.

"Mally!" Early cries as I come through the door and he swings me off my feet. He has the same beard he had when I was little, only now it has grey in it, and the braid down his back is thinner.

He claims that Mally is some ancient form of Molly, and he's fond of ancient things. He travels the world and takes pictures of old stuff and people pay him for the photos. Pay a lot, though you'd never know. By some standards, he owns nothing. But, he quickly adds, he owes nothing, too.

"Where's Candace?"

Why does he ask that first thing? "At her house," I say. "And she's fine," I add, because that'll be his next question. I don't tell him about her disappointment with art class. Sometimes it's just best to avoid the negative with Uncle Early: his inner Eeyore has a keen nose. I *could* tell him about the RECYCLE collage; he'd like that.

But he moves the conversation on with: "And how are you?"

"Fine, too. High school's going to be good..."

Uncle Early can tell I'm about to go on, and he puts up his hand to stop me. "Come and help with those old things of Grand's. And you can tell me all about it while we work."

"Now *there's* a plan!" says Mom, coming into the kitchen. "If I trip over those boxes of pictures one more time, I'll throw them out, I swear!"

"But they're Grand's *photographs*," I say. Can't quite believe Mom would throw them out.

She looks right at me. "Molly, they're not *photographs*. *Photographs* are pictures you take yourself, of people you know and love, and you put them in places where you'll see them and be reminded of them. Grand's *pictures* are reprints of old eight-by-tens, of people she didn't know and never met." My mother is breathing heavily, and she turns away and begins to haul dinner pieces out of the fridge.

"I've always wondered if you were a bit…jealous…of her," I say, pretty much in a whisper because I've never thought this aloud.

"Jealous?" She turns back, eyes round.

Uncle Early grabs my elbow. "We're going to get on that right now, Tessie," he says to Mom. "Right now, yes, those pictures – *photographs* – on the wall. This way, Molly." And he pulls me from the room.

The boxes, three of them, are just outside the Hole, the small and overflowing storage room that Mom likes to think she'll make something of someday.

Early thrusts one box into my arms and picks up the other two. He's looking at me with an odd, tight expression on his face. "Your mother…" he begins. Then stops.

"What?"

"There was never any reason for her to be jealous of Grand."

I've never liked how his voice goes all quiet when he's angry. I start up the stairs and he follows.

"So," he says after clearing his throat, "where are you going to hang these old ghosts?"

"Those *old ghosts* as you call them were *gods* for Grand!" I remind him. I can be angry, too. Though it's always difficult to be angry with Early for any length of time.

"Yes," he says, "I remember well. Mad–as–a–hatter Grand! I think she used to leave out plates of fruitcake for them as offerings." He pulls a frame from a box. "Here she is! Red carpet for this one. Greta Garbo. Grand always had her in a corner by herself, because the Great Garbo was known for..."

I interrupt. "I know, I know! She was known for..." and I try to get the accent right "*...vhanting to be alone.*" I point to the narrow space beside my dormer. "There."

He flips a hammer in a frightening way and catches it by the handle. He taps in a nail and I hang the picture. He stands back and shakes his head. "You and Grand," he says, "both besieged by dreams of theatre."

"More than dreams!" I protest.

Early reaches into the box and pulls out another. "Maybe for you, more than dreams."

"What do you mean?" I put out my hand to hold the picture so he can hammer.

Tap, tap. "My mother never so much as *saw* backstage."

Through my mind flashes what I saw earlier: grey back curtains, red velvet, the guts. And I take in that he's used a word I never hear him or Mom use: "mother." Grand is always Grand, never "mother."

"What do you mean?" I ask.

Early slips this next picture over the nail. Sir Laurence Olivier. Then he stands, hammer held loosely by his thigh, and he sighs. It's that grown-up I've-said-too-much sigh. I haven't heard it for a while now.

"What?"

He taps in another nail without asking me where I want it. "It's like this," he says. "Your grandmother...adored the theatre. Drama. She was a big fan of drama. But no." His voice drifts to a whisper. "No, I don't believe she was ever actually on stage."

He hangs up Vivien Leigh next to Laurence, where she belongs. "But you knew that, didn't you?" he asks me.

There's that gust of wind again, and I remember that cottonwood, and suddenly I know what it would have looked like falling to the ground. What a thud it would have made, on that windy Sunday morning.

He's looking as if he wishes he'd never opened his mouth. "She lived in make-believe. She could forget about reality. Often did. Would forget to pack a lunch for us sometimes."

"But she was never on stage?"

He's pulling at his beard. "I think it would have ruined it for her."

"Ruined," I repeat.

"It was a fantasy for her. Nothing more. She couldn't have taken the knocks. She put it all up on a pedestal, so high. Unreachable."

Tap, tap. Judy Garland is on the wall. "The problem with pedestals," Early goes on, "is that they fall."

*Sort of like cottonwoods*, I want to say, but can't get the words out. I wonder what he means by "the knocks."

He picks up another frame and laughs, a relieved laugh. "This one!" he says. "This fellow made her *laugh*. The others she held in awe, but this one..." He holds up a picture of Edgar Bergen with his dummies: Charlie McCarthy in his tails and monocle and Mortimer Snerd, big-nosed and goofy. "She grew up with his radio show, every Sunday night. He was a great ventriloquist." Early looks for a place to hang the photo, and I motion to the other side of the dormer. Somehow, Edgar and Charlie and Mortimer don't quite fit with the others, with Vivien and Laurence, Garbo and Garland.

Early hangs the photo, then sits on the edge of the bed, looking tired. "I always hoped she'd come out of that and throw away all these and put up pictures of you, like a normal grandmother."

I pick up the hammer he set down, and tap in a nail. "Everyone has a normal grandmother. I'm glad I had Grand."

But the words sound hollow, even to me, and I wonder suddenly: what do I really know about my grandmother? I've always thought of her as *knowing* the people in the photographs, or having met with them, at least. Grand always had such stories about them.

Is that all they were? Just stories?

# 5
# So Bright

*A*very – Candace's mother – answers the door next morning. Avery has her own sewing and yarn store, and she's written a whole series of craft books. LESSONS FOR EVERYONE, says the sign in her store window. I try not to stare at her belly, but she really does take up more room than ever before.

"Molly!" she says, and takes my wrist. "I have something I want you to see." In her hands she holds a bundle of soft denim with wide straps and bright snaps. "I've been designing this all week. Here, Candace, help me." She holds it over her head.

"Designing all week and you can't even put it on by yourself," says Candace.

Avery doesn't say anything about the anger in Candace's voice, but I notice her jaw tighten as she works with Candace to tug it into place. "It's my baby carrier," she says, although I'd already figured as much.

Avery stuffs a teddy bear into it. "See how it works? With pockets for fingers and toes, to keep the babe out of the way while I work."

"Out of the way," echoes Candace.

A shadow passes Avery's face. "I didn't mean it like *that*," she says. "I meant *safe*, from scissors and sewing machine."

But Candace has scooped up her lunch bag and knapsack, and leaves me to help. Avery raises her arms over her head and I pull. Her voice is muffled inside the denim. "With this baby on the way, Candace seems to think I want *her* out of the way." She folds away the carrier on a shelf. "You'd better go. I've made you late." She looks so sad. I wish I could say something to her, but I don't know what. Instead, I run after Candace, which isn't easy with those long legs of hers. I don't catch up until we're almost to the school.

"Do you ever talk to her about the baby?" I gasp, slipping through the door as it closes.

Candace turns to me so quickly that I have to step back. I can feel the door handle in my back.

"Four years ago," she begins, and her words are stretched tight, "the fish store began to sell sushi supplies on Fridays."

I nod. Yes, I've often shared Candace and Avery's sushi nights. What's *that* got to do with her mom being pregnant?

She goes on. "That used to be when we talked. We'd roll the tuna and rice and wasabi…"

"Candace!" I interrupt. "I know what you do for Friday supper!"

"Well, not anymore," she says.

"What do you mean?"

"I mean, one Friday in June my mother puts this thing on the table, with a burner under it. I said, 'What's this?' and she said, 'Fondue.' 'Fondue? We don't do fondue!' I said. 'We do now,' she said."

As she is speaking, Candace has begun to stalk off to her locker. I half run to keep up, to catch her words. She alternates her own voice with a silly high-pitched voice that is nothing like Avery's low monotone. People are staring. But it doesn't seem to bother her.

"So," she says, "I asked my mom, 'Since when?' Since when do we have fondue on Friday?' and she said, 'Since I can't eat sushi, uncooked fish.' 'Can't eat sushi?' I said. Then Mom said, '*You* can't eat uncooked fish when *you're* pregnant' as if *I'm* the one stupid enough to go and get pregnant!"

Candace isn't paying attention to the gawking faces. She continues with her story. "'What do you mean '*you*'?' I asked my mom. Then it hit me. 'You mean *YOU!*' I said to her."

Candace wrestles with her lock. "That's how she told me — told she's going to have a baby...and I'm going to be a sister! And she thinks I'm going to sit with her after that and chow down *fondue!*" She slams open her locker and grabs books.

"She had to tell you somehow."

"Not like that!" Another slam of the door.

"Then how?"

"I don't know. But not like that!" And she's off.

"Still," I call after her. "I think you need to talk."

"She talks all the time! Talk, talk, talk..." Candace calls over her shoulder. She seems to have forgotten we're in the same class. I trail after.

"What does she say?"

We're in class now, and she takes her seat with a thump.

"What does your mom say?" I repeat.

Candace finally looks right at me. "Nothing." Her shoulders slump. "Absolutely nothing." Hair falls across her face. "Nothing that makes any sense."

I see Julian's shadow friend looking at us from across the room. I'm glad Candace doesn't see: his face is so full of concern, it's almost embarrassing.

Mr. Pritchard calls the roll and I learn Shadow's name: Caleb. He smiles at me, just a regular smile.

# 6
# Pig Baby

For the second week of school, Ms. Tanaka has set the classroom as a stage. "I've invited an audience." A girl named Annie groans.

"It's not that bad," says Ms. Tanaka. "They're your class-mates. They're not here to poke fun at you."

"Are you gonna check their bags for rotten vegetables?" Julian asks.

Katherine speaks up. "Ya – put 'em through the vegetable detector."

There's laughter, but Annie doesn't look at ease, and not for the first time I wonder what she's doing here. This class is an elective, and it doesn't seem healthy for her to put herself through this.

Ms. Tanaka checks her watch. "I've invited Mr. Kerrigan's art class. They'll be here any minute."

That means Candace will be watching. I'd been feeling

just a nudge of that jittery feeling — the Entrance Hall Feeling, First Day at Blue Point High, is how I've been thinking of it — and the feeling is gone when I think of Candace. Instead, I feel a gentle warmth and I smile at Annie. *It'll be okay. Really.* She frowns back at me. Sometimes telepathy just doesn't cut it.

There's the sound of footsteps down the hall, and a voice. "Now people! Line up!" Is that the art teacher, Mr. Kerrigan? No wonder Candace isn't too happy about him.

The door opens and they file in marching. I salute Candace — which seems appropriate — and receive a grimace in return as they sit neatly in rows on the floor with hardly a word from Mr. Kerrigan. Ms. Tanaka looks astonished.

"It's like performance art, isn't it?" she says. Mr. Kerrigan looks blankly at her, and I look at Candace, whose look has given way to one of complete misery. Ms. Tanaka gives a brief introduction then calls for Julian, who has chosen to perform a monologue.

"I wrote it myself, if 'wrote' is the word to describe what I've done. Really, it's what I call a goofologue." When his mouth opens next, it's only gibberish that comes out...but no...wait...there's rhythm, inflection, some pattern to it. Every face in the room is turning to smile because we all know exactly what he's saying. And it's not only his mouth speaking: it's those golden eyes and his hands and his feet and every part of him.

"Rubber face," someone behind me whispers. "Rubber *man!*" Katherine mutters. I look at Candace and can tell she's completely forgotten Mr. Kerrigan. By the time Julian's come to the end, no one can hear him over the laughter, and Ms. Tanaka is wiping tears, she's laughing so hard. Mr. Kerrigan smiles. Hesitantly.

Then we're up, with *Grace's Garden*, our dialogue. Katherine is Grace, with a wide-brimmed, floppy sun hat, incongruous with her eyebrow ring. "This is a change of pace," she says apologetically to the audience, and with a nod in Julian's direction. She sets up a few flowerpots while I take my place, leaning over the makeshift potting table. I hear her take in a deep breath and let it out slowly. So she's a bit nervous. That surprises me. Especially after Julian, I'm ready to go.

Another deep breath. "Okay," she whispers.

I begin, and I have a lot to say. All Ms. Tanaka said when we showed her our selection was a few words to Katherine. "It's not easy being the silent one on stage. There are no words to hang on to." She didn't say anything to me about being the one with everything to say, and now, here's me, and timing is everything. Katherine's character, Grace, has to speak at just the right moment, and I have to seize the words from her mouth and make it all happen. I can feel my heart pound, but with excitement.

She does speak at exactly the moment – yes, Katherine! – and

I take it from there. Inside me, I can hear Mr. Roman's voice: *Molly, project!* And Miss Rose, my old dance teacher: *With your eyes, Molly, hold them with your eyes.* And Grand. I've always heard Grand in the back of my mind. She's in there somewhere. I know she is. What does Early know?

It's better than we ever rehearsed. It flows, all my words, and each of Grace's significant looks as she trolls along with the trowel and pots and soil. Oh, Grand would know exactly what this was like. I know she would. The applause is loud, and I believe I can hear Candace, her hand rhythm just slightly off.

"A convincing bit of gardening," Ms. Tanaka comments when the applause comes to an end. She touches my shoulder briefly. "Good work, Molly Gumley." I squirm under the Gumley word.

"Thanks," I mutter, and find a place to sit.

The performance ends with the final bell and, with a word from Mr. Kerrigan, the art class lines up.

"Do you have to find a partner and hold hands?" Julian asks in a not-so-low voice. Students in both classes laugh, even those lined up like kindergarten kids.

Candace gives a surreptitious two-finger wave. "I'll meet you outside," she mouths. Julian goose-steps alongside and escorts them from the room.

"Really, Julian," Ms. Tanaka says as he returns, but she has a hard time hiding a smile. He finds my eyes, grins, winks. I do like this guy, and I have a feeling there's something he likes about me, too.

Julian follows me to my locker and holds my books while I replace the combination lock. Then trails me to where Candace waits by the maple. "That Mr. K is an uptight guy," he says. He pulls a chocolate bar from his pocket and offers each of us a piece.

Candace nods. "Yeah," is all she says, before popping the chocolate into her mouth. Several times she breathes deeply, as if she's going to speak again, but she doesn't. Finally, she manages, "He is." Then she stops, bites her lip, looks at me.

"Go on," says Julian. "You've got a whole bunch of other words about him inside your skull. I can tell." He nibbles at his chocolate. But Candace just shakes her head with that miserable look that's becoming almost familiar.

"Have you noticed how people have been adding to your RECYCLE collage?" he says. "You started something with that, you know."

But Candace doesn't even smile. She doesn't want to be cheered up.

"Maybe Mr. Kerrigan has some collage ideas..." Julian starts to say in a teasing voice, but Candace's look of instant fury cuts him off.

"Sorry," he says. "I just thought, being the art teacher and all, he might have an idea."

"The man has *no* ideas," says Candace.

"I like when you're mad," says Julian, with a grin. "I'm not going to disagree with you. More chocolate?" And he holds out the bar.

"No, thanks," says Candace. "Molly and I have to go." And she pulls at me.

"But we just got here," says Julian amiably, holding the chocolate out to me.

"I like chocolate," I say before Candace runs away.

Candace reaches out, breaks off a piece and hands it to me, then pulls me along away from the school. I look back to see Julian standing there, a bewildered expression on his face, and with a slight shaking of his head from side to side.

We're halfway down the block, and she begins to grumble. "I don't see why he has to follow us around all the time."

"Who?" I ask, even though I think I know what she's going to say.

"Julian! He's become a part of my elbow."

"What's wrong with that?" *And why does she think it's her elbow and not mine?* Is it my imagination, or does she begin to speed up?

"I just don't want boys in my life right now," she says. "For once I wish we were in a private girls' school."

"What's wrong with boys?"

"They grow up to be men," she says, in almost a wail. She slows a bit and her voice softens. "It would all be so much easier without men in the world."

"Are we talking about you or your mom here?" I ask, coming to a full stop.

"Well, Mom *acts* as if there are no men in the world...with her Virgin Mary routine."

"She's never going to tell you who the father is?"

"What does it matter," says Candace.

"She is due at Christmastime," I say.

Candace snorts, then quickly hiccups. "Funny thing is..." Another hiccup..."I don't remember her even dating anybody this year."

I don't remind Candace how often she's away from home, at my house. Sometimes it seems like for days.

"What does she say when you ask?"

Hiccup. "I don't."

"You don't?"

"Nope." She holds her breath, her cheeks grow like Dizzy Gillespie's, but she can't stop the next hiccup, and her ribs heave. "Oh!" she gasps as her breath explodes. "I wish we could just stay the same as it's always been, just me and her."

"What about *your* dad?" I ask.

"What about him?" Hiccup.

We don't talk about our fathers often. We were the two kids in kindergarten who didn't have fathers. By second grade we had it worked out, and while the other kids created Father's Day cards, we spent the June afternoon painting and colouring. One year, Candace made a Mother's Day #2 card.

I usually made a card for Uncle Early. But even though we had that in common — no fathers — there was a difference. There was the 'wouldn't' and 'couldn't' of it: my father had gone down a highway on a motorcycle, and now he couldn't be around. Candace's father had gone who-knows-where, and he wouldn't be around. Sometimes I felt bad about the difference, and other times I felt bad about the sameness. Most of the time I reminded myself that there was nothing I could do about it.

"Have you really never wanted him around?" I ask her. That's what she's always said.

"He's never been around," she says now.

*But that's different, isn't it?* "Why does your mom never say anything about him?'

She shrugs, and I can't tell whether she wants to say something or not. "Don't you ask?"

"I don't need to know. I don't ask about stuff I don't need to know."

"How can you not need to know?"

No answer.

"Well, you must *want* to know — it *is* happening," I remind her.

"Well, let's pretend it's not."

"That's going to be hard when you have a little person screaming in the middle of the night, crawling around in a smelly diaper in the room next to yours. Or is the baby going to share your room?"

Candace shudders. "Maybe the baby'll be like the one in *Alice in Wonderland*, and turn into a pig and run away into the woods."

# 7
# Singing In The Rain

onday morning. The day Ms. Tanaka is going to draw names for the December variety show. If my name is chosen, I might do a monologue, or a song, a piece from *Rent* maybe. I enjoyed singing in *The Wizard of Oz*.

I do a quick Charleston step on the sidewalk – something Grand taught me so long ago now – and hurry on to Candace's house. The air is a little colder, even with a vest over my hoodie.

Reality check: there must be dozens and dozens of names in Ms. Tanaka's big jar, and only ten people can be lucky. Still. It's fun to think about. Maybe I can dress as a man – Gene Kelly or Fred Astaire – and do a dance number. I can find an old fedora...I grab a bus pole and sing out *"I'm haaaaaappy again..."*

I catch sight of Candace and wave to her. *"With a smile on my face..."*

"Who are you?" Candace calls as she nears, a smile on her own face.

"I'm Gene Kelly. I'm singing in the rain."

Candace falls into step with me. "That's what I'm gonna try to do today."

"Singing in the rain?"

"Being happy in art class, yeah. Mom's trying to convince me to see the positive."

"Which is?"

"I've been thinking," Candace says, "maybe I just need to ask Mr. Kerrigan questions and remind him why he's doing this. He mentioned doing papier mâché in November. Maybe we could start earlier, if I ask, and he can forget about this paper lantern stuff. At least papier mâché is something like sculpture..." Her voice drifts off, but she takes a deep breath and goes on. "Maybe I *should* ask him about carving." Her tone takes on a desperate edge. "He has to know *something.*"

But I'm remembering Mr. Kerrigan and the hard time he had laughing. "I hope it works."

Before drama class there's a list posted beside Ms. Tanaka's door, and everyone is gathered to read the ten names. Actually eleven, I see, as I manage to get close. There's one name at the bottom: Julian Smart, and over it is written *wait list.* So if someone drops out, Julian fills in for them. My eyes move upward. *Names selected for Dec. 18 Variety Show.* Katherine's name is first on the list.

Mine is halfway down.

I read through again, beginning at the top. My name is there, even the Gumley part. I have a spot. I'm lucky. Maybe I'll be Gene Kelly after all, and sing in the rain.

The class passes slowly after that. I want to run to the maple, meet Candace, and tell her.

We do improvisation – stuff I usually enjoy – but the next hour is long and, as the minutes tick by, I feel as if I'm floating.

"You look like the moon that swallowed the sun!" Julian grins at me.

"Moon that swallowed the sun!" I laugh. "I like that!" It occurs to me that it would make no difference to him if his name was included with the ten, or if it wasn't on the list at all. I wonder how it can not matter to him, even as I realize that it matters to me even more than I thought possible. My mind expands as I ponder what I might do. I wasn't really serious about Gene Kelly. Besides, it feels as if it'll never rain again.

The class is finally over, and the school day. Candace is sitting with her back to the rough bark of the maple, and she doesn't move as I near. She doesn't speak either, or smile. My sense of floating tumbles; so does the smile on my face.

"What's wrong?" So much for my big moment.

Candace drags her sweater sleeve across her face as a child would. "I quit," she says.

"Quit what?"

She looks suddenly annoyed and pulls herself to her feet. "What do you think?"

"Art class," I say flatly. Julian appears from nowhere, which he's so good at.

"No," he says. "You quit Kerrigan." He emphasizes the teacher's name. Candace gives a half smile. "You can't quit art just because of that guy," he goes on. "There are other art teachers."

"I already asked," says Candace, speaking to Julian. I seem to have dropped off the edge of the earth at this point. "I asked my counsellor and she says the art classes are full, and as an elective there's only a couple of spaces left in guitar. So I'll be strumming until next term."

Julian's doing his grinning-and-nodding thing. "That's cool. Learning a little campfire guitar is good."

"You think?" Candace can't be won over that quickly.

"Of course!" he says. "Artists need to understand more than one art form."

Candace is staring at him. "You might be right," she says slowly. "Maybe..."

"Then there's Molly's big news," he says, and before I can get a word in, he blurts it out: "She's in the December variety show! What do you think of *that?*"

Candace lets out a squeal as an answer. "That's wonderful, Molly!" She gives me a hug, and Julian pats her on the back instead of me.

That was my news to share, not his.

"Caleb's at volleyball practice," he says, as he falls into step with us on the way home. "Say, do you have a guitar? I could stop by and show you a few things – help you get caught up with the rest of the class."

"That would be good," says Candace. "I'm going to feel so behind when I start next week."

"We can fix that," says Julian. And he begins to tell her about the parts of a guitar and the frets and strings...and I tune it out. At the corner to Candace's house, they turn, Julian mid-explanation. I stand and wait to see how long it'll take them to realize I'm not with them. At the foot of her driveway, Julian suddenly looks around and sees me. "See you tomorrow!" he calls out to me.

Sure. Tomorrow.

# 8

# Inside Out

Wednesday afternoon, I discover I'm missing my sheet of math problems, though I'm certain I tucked it into the pages of my textbook. I'd planned to do my homework before dinner so I can watch *The Sound of Music*, and my plans are ruined.

I pull everything out of my knapsack, and from under my bed. I even think of searching the Hole, but it can't be there. I haven't been able to get into that closet room in months. I put my clothes on and head down the street.

She's in her room," says Avery, picking at several different coloured threads that ride on the top of her belly. I can see the soft bulge of her belly button poking at the jersey of her tunic. Pretty soon she's gonna be inside out.

I start up the stairs and she gives me a funny look. "Didn't

Candace tell you?" she asks. "She's moving into the room over the garage."

I try to think if Candace told me. Or why she wouldn't tell me.

The garage door is off the laundry room, and I step down into the cold gloom of the garage with its cement floor and murky light from one long and narrow window.

"The light switch is here," Avery reminds me.

I can't imagine what this is going to be like in winter. All the way down these old stairs and across the cold floor every time she needs a snack or the toilet. I push the door open, and remember coming up here to explore when we were in Grade 2/3, flashlights in hand, poking around all the junk that Avery and Candace's grandparents and who-knows-who collected for years. I remember how we'd gone screaming out of the room and down the stairs, our hair all sticky with cobweb. Now Candace is going to live here.

I find her, hair tied up, kneeling beside a stack of boards. The stack is usually her bed. Empty drawers are scattered about, though I don't see any clothes, and the wall right by the stairs is piled to the ceiling with boxes. They must be filled with all the junk she had to clean out. The place is still dusty, and the webs are so thick they look false.

"We could have a Halloween party," I say.

"I need you to help with my mattress. Mom's no use at all," she says, ignoring my reference to the spiderwebs.

We go downstairs, into the house, then upstairs. The trip back, with her mattress between us, is a long one. Her mom is nowhere to be seen, and Candace mutters a couple words I haven't heard her use before. Back over the garage, we let it drop to the floor, and Candace sneezes as dust flies.

"Where's the vacuum?" I ask.

"Broken. Getting it fixed is low priority for Mom."

"I'll get ours." I'd really like to get out of here. It feels so uncomfortable with Avery and Candace.

She shakes her head. "It's okay."

"No, really." I head for the door.

"Really," she says. "I'll get the broom later." There go my plans for escape.

"It's going to be sort of lonely in here," I say.

She motions toward the wall. "Mom's just on the other side. The baby can have my room – it's bigger than the work-room Mom was going to turn into a nursery. And here..." Candace waves her arms around the room "it's *my* place." She looks so sad, it shocks me.

So why don't I stop? Why do I keep pushing? Because the next words out of my mouth are, "I'd feel weird in a room this huge." Which is really an odd thing to say. I mean, huge rooms have never made me feel weird, so why do I even say this?

When Candace speaks, her words are slow, as if she's speaking to an old deaf person. "I need room for my carving, and I've begun to collect things to make collages at home. This is going to be my studio."

That's when I notice the corner, set up with a work table. While she hasn't had time to put together her bed, or even her drawers, she's made a wall rack for all her chisels or whatever they are. There's an entire row of them, each with a clearly marked home, and screws and nails are sorted into small plastic containers that are probably supposed to be in Avery's kitchen. There's a shelf with too many shades of craft paint, and tin cans nailed to the walls for brushes.

She seems to read my mind. "I haven't needed the bed set up. And I only need jeans and a few shirts."

"An assortment of underwear and matching socks is always good."

"They don't have to match," she says quickly.

"And it's kind of dark in here." Why am I in such a fighting mood?

She motions to the stack of books that almost block the window overlooking the driveway. "The window behind that is bigger than the window in your room!" She says this in such a way that I can't say a word back, and she takes a book from a pile. Post-it notes are stuck in the pages. "I've decided to teach myself," she says. She begins to read titles, about carving and art. I pull out one about trees. "Might as well start at the beginning," she says as she notices it in my hands.

Then there's a whole other stack. *Childbirth Naturally.*

*Expecting a Child*. I pick up one: *Everything You Need To Know About Childbirth*. "I thought you were going to pretend it's not happening?"

Candace frowns. "I should know something about it. Maybe I'll ask Mom if I can go to that prenatal class with her. Though she says 'no' to everything lately."

I pick up the *Naturally* book. The woman on the cover makes Avery look like a grandmother. I turn the pages. *Fear of pain*, I read. "You've read this?" Candace nods quickly. Before I close the book, I catch the words *Your child is on the other side of your pain*. Now what does that mean? The pile of books sways as I replace it. There are times I really wonder about all this growing up stuff. Like it's a big treat to become a woman.

"If I were you, I'd just keep on pretending."

"You're not me, are you?" she snaps. She picks up an oversized art book and holds it.

I shiver suddenly. "It's cold up here."

"Mom said she'd buy me an electric heater. Besides..." she pulls the book tightly to her chest and speaks over the top of it. "Some of us have to suffer for our art."

"Hey!" I say. "I'm supposed to be the dramatic one here." But Candace isn't acting. Her voice is more real than I've ever heard and though my voice is loud, inside I'm shrinking fast. I'm not even sure what she means. Or why we're pushing at each other like this.

She goes to her worktable, and rattles around among her tools.

"See you," I say, and wish I had something in my hands to hide behind, too.

I'm almost home when I remember the math. Mr. Pritchard's a nice guy, yes, but I'm learning that the Winnie-the-Pooh aspect of his personality gets stuck in Rabbit's door if you miss an assignment. Then it becomes quite apparent that he is a Serious Teacher Preparing Young Minds for the Big World.

So it's back to Candace, and I'm thinking that she can't really have meant all that...Avery'll be at her sewing machine or desk, so I let myself in as I always have. The garage smells of oil and aging grass clippings. I switch on the light, but the bulb flickers, pops, and goes out. I'm almost at the top of the stairs when I become aware of a sound on the other side of the door: crying.

Maybe I should just go home. No, that'd be dumb.

"Candace?"

She looks up, startled, and wipes at her eyes. "Why'd you come back?" There's anger in her voice.

"I forgot — I need the math homework. I lost mine somewhere, maybe my knapsack, or..." I'm over-explaining.

Candace points to a wooden chair by the door. The math text is on top of yet more books, with a copy of the assignment tucked in the pages. My back is to her as I pull it out and tuck it in a pocket. "I'll bring it right back," I say, but all I can hear is a sniffle, and she blows her nose.

"I *knew* you needed something." But her voice isn't triumphant.

I try to ignore the mournful quality of it, and ask because I feel I should, "What's wrong?"

"Nothing." She bends over and rattles the sideboards of her bed as if she just might put the thing together herself. "Nothing you'd care about anyway!"

I'm not ready for that. It's not fair. I'm her friend. I care. "How can you say that?"

She picks up a board, fits the metal end into the headboard, and has to hammer at it with her palm. "I've had to realize something," she says. "You..." She falters. "You care about yourself and your dream. That means you don't think about others a whole lot. You've never had to work hard for anything. Whatever you want to do, Molly, it's easy for you. You have a mom and an uncle who encourage you, and teachers who tell you you're wonderful. You don't have a dad either, but at least you know a few things about yours. Me, I just have this place I'm making. And this old *junk* I collect..."

I don't need to respond because she finally looks at me, and goes on with hardly a breath between.

"You come first. Molly Gumley, all the way. You might not like your name, but there it is, on the marquee – headliner Molly Gumley. The rest of us are small stuff. You don't listen to me. You don't need to..." She is out of breath now, but still not finished. She pushes the other side of the bed into the headboard. "Do you remember when you discovered my mom was pregnant?"

"Of course." And she thinks I don't listen. I still remember Avery opening the front door wearing the biggest red sweatshirt I'd ever seen.

"You probably think it was the time she answered the door in that red shirt, don't you?"

I say nothing.

"But I told you a month before that. Do you remember?"

I'm sure she hadn't said a word about her mom before that.

"See?" she shouts triumphantly, tearfully. "You don't hear me. Mom hasn't heard me in months. Mr. Kerrigan didn't hear me, but he's a numbskull, and Mom has her problems. But *you*...you're supposed to be my best friend!"

I'm trying to think of something to say.

"Just go," she says, and reaches for the long screws that hold the pieces together. They're on the floor just beyond her grasp and I move to pick them up for her, but she drops the bed pieces and gets them first. "I can do this," she says, and it sounds as if her teeth are clenched.

9

# Proof

ruth is, I think on the way home, that I can't deny her words. I do think a lot about myself and what I want. A kid with focus, I've been called. "A little driven," Uncle Early once said. "Not a bad thing, so long as the wind pushing you is a good one."

"You look like the cat's got your soul!"

I hadn't seen Early sitting on the front steps by the hydrangea. Now I smell the sweet smell of his pipe and wonder how I missed it.

"It's 'cat got your tongue,'" I correct him.

"I know." Early tilts his head, scrutinizing me. "Seems it's got more than your tongue, though."

I sit next to him. "Candace hates me."

"Yeah?"

"She does. Just now, at her house, she told me to leave."

"She doesn't hate you. She's just telling you that, as a

friend, you stink."

I say nothing.

"How do I know this? Because I've watched you, and you're a lot like me," he adds in a rueful tone. "You're into your own thing."

"That's what Candace said. But being an actor takes a lot of work," I defend myself. Someone has to.

"It does," he agrees. "But you won't get where you want to go by yourself."

I frown. "That's not true. How else can I get there? That's what everyone says, 'Only *you* can get there or do that.'"

"Yeah, I know what they say, whoever 'they' are. I'd like to run into them someday – run *over* them maybe if the Bug was willing! But you're not going to get there without friends. That's all I'm saying."

Early looks as if he's tired of the subject. "I know one thing," he says. "A soulmate, such as Candace is for you, well, they don't turn up too often. Do something, Mally. Do something to prove your friendship."

He stops, and puffs on his pipe.

Something to prove my friendship, eh?


First block of the day is Humanities. Today we're supposed to be working on research skills in the library and we're on line. I search for 'woodworking.' Can't find anything. 'Carving...' How about 'art'? 'Art Schools,' our area. Nothing local of course, but in the city. That's not too far. Here's one: Arts Unlimited. And a phone number. Sculpture and carving is listed.

"How's the research?" It's the librarian, over my shoulder.

"I think I've got it."

The name is familiar; I think it's the place Grand sent me to drama camp that one year. It's an hour away in the city, it's expensive, and it's good. After that, Mom said local dance classes would have to do. I can still remember Grand finding the newspaper article about Ms. Tanaka coming to the high school. "*Now* you'll have a real drama teacher – a professional," she'd said. Candace wasn't so lucky.

At lunch, I phone the number. "Do you have a carving class? Wood carving?"

"Our Fall classes began last week."

"I have a friend who needs to take this class."

"Has she done any carving? This is not a beginners' class."

"Her grandpa taught her. I think she's quite good."

"Is she at least fourteen years old?"

"Yes."

The voice pauses. "We do have two spots left. Can she be here by four o'clock?"

It's too close now. "We'll be there."

"And how will you be paying?"

Hadn't thought of that. But I have my savings for Dogwood Players' Camp, and I can replenish the account before summer. I can go to the bank, which leaves just the how-are-we-going-to-get-there problem. Enter Avery. She'll have to be in on this.

Then there's the other problem: will Candace even speak to me?

After school, I go to the maple, hoping Candace will walk by. She does. "What are you doing here?"

Then Avery pulls up.

"What is *she* doing here?"

Avery motions for us to open the passenger door. "Jump in. I'm kidnapping you."

I like how this is turning out. I begin to laugh, but Candace isn't buying. She looks suspicious and hesitates. I start toward the door, but she pushes past me and slides into the front seat beside her mother. "What do you mean 'kidnapping'?"

"I mean 'jump in,'" Avery repeats.

I crawl into the back seat. The locks click as Avery pushes a button. She grins. "See? I am kidnapping you, spiriting you away to a place of wonder."

"What place?"

"You'll see. Do you want to come along, Molly?" Avery asks, as if she hasn't spoken already to my mother. "Or shall I drop you by your house?"

"I'm sure she has something to do at home," Candace mutters.

I cut her off. "I'm coming."

"Good." Avery wiggles in her seat to find a more comfortable position for her belly.

"Is it a long drive?" Candace asks.

"Just into the city." An hour away. More in rush hour.

"What if you go into early labor?"

"What do you know about early labor?" Avery raises a brow.

Candace ignores the question. "What if you do?"

"That's not going to happen...but we'll be closer to the hospital, I guess."

"Just where *are* we going?"

"I'm not saying."

Candace stares out the window. "Poor Baby," she mutters. "Your mom's a nut."

"Thank you," says Avery. "I'll take that as a compliment. I've never aspired to sanity." She fiddles with radio stations, trying to find the right one. She stops at a popular station. "And I'm so glad you've decided to speak to your sibling."

Candace reddens.

"Mom!" she calls out over the sound of guitars and bass. "What's with the music?"

"You don't like it?" Avery is at a red light, and is tapping the steering wheel with her fingernails. Even in the rain, her window is open a bit. She says she's too hot all the time: 'That's what comes of being an incubator.' The young man in the truck next to her hears the music and looks over in amazement. Avery waves to him. "Gee, he must think I'm ancient. Maybe I do have the bass cranked." She fiddles with a knob, and we're off again.

"Okay," says Candace as we near the city. "Where is it we're going?"

Avery only nods and smiles in a most annoying way. I can tell she's enjoying this. Candace, on the other hand, is really building on this storm-cloud characteristic I've never met until recently. She hasn't said a word to me or even looked in my direction, and I can't help but wonder just how she's going to feel when the truth is in front of her.

Just before the last bridge downtown, Avery pulls a quick left, then right, to an area under the bridge. It's an old industrial area but now the buildings are bright and we can hear live music from the nearby market. Avery turns down a few streets that are more like lanes, and stops in front of a large window. In the window there are clay objects and wood. Paintings hang on backdrops. The name of the place is over the window in swirly, rusted metal letters: ARTS UNLIMITED.

Avery makes a presenting motion with her hands. "Ta da! Here you are!" She peeks at her watch. "The wood carving class started five minutes ago. Better get in there!"

Candace peers through the car window, looks up at the letters, then at the window, like a little kid checking the pictures to figure out the words, then back to her mom wonderingly, back up to the name. Suddenly, her head swivels to me. "You knew about this?"

Avery says, "This was all Molly's idea."

Candace doesn't apologize for her earlier grumpiness. All she says is a soft "thanks" that drags a smile with it; if she was on stage, that smile couldn't be seen by anyone, even in the front row. It's an up-close thing, Candace's smile, and I feel lucky. Just in time I remember the envelope of twenty-dollar bills I got from the bank, but Avery guesses what I'm up to.

"I've taken care of it," she says.

Candace looks from her mom to me and back again. "Thanks. Both of you." She hurries in, but as she nears the door, she stops and comes back, opens the car door with a gust of rain and wind, and throws her ropy arms around her mom's shoulders. "Thank you, THANK you, THANK YOU!" she says, leaving Avery astonished and gasping. And not displeased. And me wondering when's my turn.

"Oh my!" says Avery, swiping at her eyes with her sleeves. "I've forgotten how I bawl about everything when I'm pregnant." She swipes again, even as fresh tears come.

Then it is my turn for the Candace-skinny-arm-treatment. I feel just a bit like a hero. Hero Molly. *Here's your proof, Early: I can be a good friend.*

# 10

# Out There

**M**om pops her head through the doorway. "I've got just what you need," she says, and plops a dish in front of me.

"I'm going over my lines for the audition tomorrow."

"Of course," she says. "That's why I brought you pistachio nuts — they're good for the memory."

I laugh. "Mom, I can say my lines forwards, backwards, and up and down!"

"And pistachios taste good," she adds. She leaves and returns with a steaming mug. "Tea, always good for the nerves. *I* think," she adds.

"Are you saying I need something for nerves? First, my memory is going, then my nerves are not good?"

She rumples my hair and sits beside me. "I'm just looking for a reason to come and talk with you, and say the old 'break a leg' thing. I think you'll be fine. Really."

The way she adds that word 'really' pokes at me for some reason. "You don't think I'll be fine."

She looks a bit startled, stands up and moves away, over to the dresser, to those photos that she set up. "Well," she pauses. "You've always had so much confidence that you will be, so why wouldn't you?" She picks up the photo of me as Dorothy in a gingham dress. Then the one of me in a tutu and a grin at age four. I know it's a favourite of hers.

"You knew about Grand, didn't you?" I ask. "You knew about her never being on stage."

Mom puts down the photos. "I knew," she says.

"Why did you never tell me?

"I guess," she begins, "that if I knew then what I know now, I might have told you all along. But even when you were little, you'd already had such big realities to face – losing your dad, living with a grieving mom. I remember watching you and Grand play dress-up, and it was such an innocent fantasy, I thought. Seemed so easy at the time. I was glad for those moments of laughter. You two would drape a curtain and put on a show; I would be the audience and applaud for as long and loud as I could." Her voice takes on a musing quality. "It was fun," she says. "Just fun. It never occurred to me that it was what you might want to do with your life, that you would take it seriously. If it had, I might have said something. Grand would tell you stories, I'm not even sure where she got them. Stories of stage life, almost as if she'd been there. The stories sounded marvelous, really."

There's that word again.

Mom takes Grand's old feather boa from where it sits across the top of my mirror, and drapes it around her own neck. "But they weren't her stories. They weren't a part of her life. Like these old pictures she gave you, hanging on your walls."

I want to tell Mom that these pictures are a part of my life, though. Really.

Mom looks into the mirror and fiddles with the boa, flicks it over a shoulder, looking slightly amused. "What do you think?" she asks.

"It's not you, Mom."

"Not even a little?"

"Not this much," I say, and hold up my first finger and thumb and press them together.

She unwraps the boa and replaces it over the mirror. "Good," she says. "That's how I want it."

I'm surprised how many people there are outside the drama class at three o'clock. The low-ceilinged brown hallway is filled with people and with end-of-day smells — even perspiration, which reminds me of the gym stage at middle school. I thought I'd gotten away from that.

"Oh! I'm so nervous I could wet my pants! Right here!" The girl who squawks those words is tall – maybe Grade 11 or 12 – and skinny as a noodle. With her thick flappy ponytails, she looks like Jar Jar Binks, but there is something appealing about her, even attractive. Maybe her bluntness: Who has the nerve to admit they're about to pee their pants? She catches my eye and grins. "Know what I mean?" she asks.

I shake my head. I don't think I'd be here if I felt like that. "Let me know if I should move to the other side of the hall."

Julian materializes from the moving swarm. "Hey," he greets me. "You'll be trying for the role of Maria, won't you? You're a lead role kinda girl."

"What part do you want?" I ask the question even though I know the answer. And I'm right...

That big loose shrug of his. "Anything, anything at all. I just want to be a part of the show. I'll be happy doing set painting, if they'll let me."

"This way!" Ms. Tanaka's voice rises over the din and every head turns in her direction. "Auditions are on stage today, and I've asked my friend Mr. Roman from Landing Middle School to assist with casting!"

Mr. Roman is wearing his usual jeans and turtleneck, his beard trimmed in a rather Shakespearean way. He'll never change. I feel a rush of something good – as if everything will be okay. Even better. It can only be good to have him out there...

*Out there.* Funny. I've never thought of it like that before. When the stage was a platform in the gym, it wasn't *out there.* And playing dress-up with Grand was never *out there.*

Grand. My heart feels sick when I suddenly think of Grand. *It was never out there, because it wasn't real, Molly. It was all make-believe.* I fight that thought.

The spotlights shine up on stage. I take a seat with others in the darkness of the theatre. Twice I lower my seat, only to have it flip back up. I'm fumbling. It's Julian who holds it down for me as I finally sit. "Are you all right?" he whispers.

"Yeah," I say. Why wouldn't I be? I'm fine. Really.

Even in the dark, Mr. Roman has spotted me, and he's heading over. "Molly," he says with warmth, "break a leg." He touches me briefly on the shoulder, and then moves away.

I have the feeling of wanting to reach out and grab his hand. But he has to go. He's handing out scripts and Ms. Tanaka is speaking.

"You'll audition in pairs. First for the characters of the Captain and Maria." Ms. Tanaka checks her clipboard. She's all efficiency today. There's a coolness to her.

Katherine and a Grade 11 boy are up first, and they climb the steps to the stage.

Katherine does quite well, but there's a quietness to her that's just not going to work, I think. And she's so short. She'll be perfect for the oldest von Trapp girl.

Next is someone named Michael and the Jar Jar Binks

girl. On stage her voice takes me by surprise: it is deep and strong. If she's nervous now, there's no sign. I look over at Ms. Tanaka, and she's scribbling on her board. Mr. Roman is whispering to her. Two more pairs audition, including Julian. "Wish for me to break a leg," he says as he gets up from his seat.

"As if you need that," I say, but add, dutifully, "Break a leg."

It's soon obvious that Julian cannot be Captain von Trapp. There's too much jump in him, none of that stuff you'd need to march about and blow whistles. I hear Mr. Roman mutter the name of Max Detweiler, the Baroness' friend.

"Molly Gumley and Craig Bennet," Ms. Tanaka calls out next.

Craig's an older guy I've seen around. He has a grin that offsets the glacier blue-green of his eyes. He always wears a fedora. This is probably the first time I've seen him without it.

"Coming?" he asks, and I follow as we head for the stairs. He's up in two bounds. I find myself waiting until he's up, and then counting...six stairs. One, two, three. Slower. Four, five. Six. I'm at the top and I look out to where everyone sits. I have the odd sense that everything is slowing. My eyes search for the faces I know are out there. There's that *out there* thought again, and some other thought pushing hard right behind it. Not quite a thought, more a fuzzy sense of how it's been at other performances – the dance recitals, and *The Wizard of Oz*. Grand – in my mind, right beside me, *with* me — always with what I think of as her "stage smile." But she's not here this time. She might never be again.

Truth is, she never was here.

"Molly?" Craig's calling to me from the middle of the stage, and he looks puzzled. "Are you coming?"

I've never felt anything like this — this hesitation. Maybe if I move across the stage. Stage. My arms and legs feel wooden, and I have the curious feeling that the floor is pressing up as my feet step down. *May the road rise up to meet you.* Isn't that something you say when you wish a successful journey for a friend? *May the wind be at your back.* But this isn't a feeling of well-wishing. Rather, I feel all about me a cloud of...menace. I stumble towards Craig. His head is to one side, and his eyes probe mine. "Are you ready?"

I feel myself nod, though I'm not ready at all. No. Then I begin to shake my head, but too late. He's speaking his lines. He's finished. He waits.

What are my words? My mind roves frantically, but the words in my head have nothing to do with *The Sound of Music*. My feet are heavy; I can't move them. In my stomach is a terrible churning...if it's caused by butterflies, they're but-terflies with steel-toed boots. Cruel butterflies, laughing at me...can hear their voices, but not quite make out their words. Something about I'm not supposed to be here. I'm a fake...I feel so alone. Even surrounded by faces that look helpful and hopeful, I'm alone.

"Molly?" Mr. Roman's familiar voice comes to me through it all. "Molly?"

I can't respond. Inside me, there's breaking, a coming apart of pieces that I haven't even known of. I always thought there was a whole me in there. Now I know it was all glued together — only the glue isn't working now.

I have an overwhelming urge to sob. Or throw up.

"What is it?" Ms. Tanaka is coming toward me from the stairs at the far side of the stage. She nears, touches my arm. Her touch is like an electric jolt and I pull my arm away. Then I'm running, running across the stage, past Ms. Tanaka, down those stairs...six, five, four, three, two, one...out the theatre door, through an exit door, directly outside.

## 11

# Bummer

*I* run towards home. It is the only place I can think of. I run straight, not attempting to miss September puddles. My feet, in summer sandals, slap into the water, sending spray over my legs. The shock of the water feels like what I need, an awakening of sorts. I arrive at my front door, reach for the knob, but can't go in. After a moment, I go around to the backyard and find shelter under the hawthorne tree. Behind me, the house is silent, and I can hear myself breathing heavily from the running. No, not the running.

I try to assemble the broken bits. I see images: Craig's puzzled face; Ms. Tanaka's hand moving toward me; Mr. Roman's turtleneck. There's something of Grand, too, hovering. I can't see her face, but I know it's her.

Images and thoughts jostle. Words, too. Those butterfly voices. *What happened? What happened back there? On that stage you've been waiting for? You thought it was waiting for you, didn't you? And you don't even know what that was...what was it?*

Somebody's calling, a woman's voice calling a child. "Time to come in!" her voice floats over the neighbourhood. The child answers in a high voice: "Co-ming!" The sound makes me cry. I pull my knees to my chest, cross my arms over them, put my head on my arms, and sob.

"Here you are," says Candace as she sinks next to me, and puts an arm loosely over my back.

"Something happened." That much I can say.

"What?" Candace's voice is very soft.

"I'm not sure." I look up into the gnarled hawthorne tree. The little filigreed leaves are curling up for the winter months ahead, wrapping around themselves. Kind of like me, I think, huddled and shivering.

"Ms. Tanaka said you ran out. She hoped I'd find you."

I don't say anything. I'd never have thought acting would cause this sense of shame, growing, spreading through me.

"We should get out of the rain."

Candace knows where the key is, and reaches under the ceramic turtle in the garden. She unlocks the door, goes to the fridge, pours milk and prepares to make hot chocolate. I sit on the bench at the table, suddenly feeling that the back of my shirt and my shoulders are very wet. I left everything behind at school – hoodie, knapsack, books.

Candace sets a mug in front of me and sits down. She

doesn't ask again, but I know she's still waiting for an answer. I never hear the ticking of the kitchen clock as I do now. Yet it must always be that loud. A tick–tick, tick–tick that sounds as if it's slightly off. Is it always like that?

"I couldn't remember my words," I say at last when my chocolate's almost gone. "My stomach felt terrible, and my feet wouldn't move." I close my eyes.

"Sounds like stage fright." Candace's words reach right to me behind my eyelids.

"Stage fright?" Even as I repeat the words with a question mark, I know there is no doubt. I just wish she hadn't said it quite like that. The phrase is too quick, too light, to sum up all *this*.

There's a footfall outside the door and Mom is coming in. Mom, and that word of hers: "really."

*I think you'll be fine. Really. Why wouldn't you be?* Why, why, why, Mom.

"Hi, Mrs. G." Candace greets Mom loudly, to cover the silence.

"Oh, Candace." Mom sets the grocery bags on the counter. "Molly. I didn't expect you home so early." She heads out to the car for more and Candace follows to help. I'm alone for a minute. *Tick-tick, tick-tick.*

*Everyone's going to be asking 'why,' aren't they? Candace was as easy as it's gonna be. This is where easy ends.* Faces come to mind again. Mom, Ms. Tanaka, Julian, Katherine...Monday there'll be questions, and what am I going to say?

Candace is on Mom's heels through the doorway. I watch as she passes items to Mom, then gathers frozen food to take to the freezer — all the stuff I usually do. I feel as if I'm watching myself, and wonder if life will be the same. Feels as if it can't possibly be. The cottonwood has fallen. With a crash it has fallen right across my path — missed me by inches, but I'm not at all sure I feel lucky, because there it is, blocking my way.

"Molly?" Mom is staring at me. "You're not helping."

There it is: the question 'why?'

A puzzled look passes over her face. "Wasn't today your audition day?"

"It was," is all I say. Before Mom or Candace can say anything, I climb the stairs and close myself in my bedroom.

*Maybe I can stay here forever.*


Candace must have told Mom.

The smell of supper wafts upstairs. Mom always counts on the healing aroma of good food, but this time it's not going to work. I'm going to stay on my bed, sitting, my pillow pulled up on to my lap. I'm holding it just like I used to hold my old stuffed rabbit, I realize, and for a second I push it away from myself. But no one else is in this room, it's my room, and I pull it back toward me, and bury my eyes into the flannel.

Mom's not singing as she often does in the kitchen, nor is the radio on. Except for the sounds of clearing up, it's quiet.

Then she goes to the piano and picks out a tune. Next, I hear a bite of TV news, then off. A rattle of newspaper.

The phone rings, a sharp sound, and I hear Mom's voice, then her footsteps on the stairs. I put the pillow aside.

"It's Early," she says. As she hands the phone to me, she adds, "There's cannelloni downstairs." *Cannelloni's gonna win me over, Mom, and make it all go away.*

"How'd it go?" Early's voice jars me.

"Not too good," I mumble.

There's a silence as he interprets my words. When he next speaks, his voice booms more, with that joviality that some adults fake when they're scared for you. "Come on! I'll bet you blew them away!"

"No," I say. "I didn't blow anyone away. I...froze."

"Well." His voice softens. "Get back up there, Mally girl!"

I say nothing.

"Bummer," he says, Eeyore coming through. Then he asks for Mom.

I find her downstairs and give her the phone. The cannelloni is sitting on the counter. I take one, and bite into it. Tastes like the sole of a shoe. I push it off the plate into the trash and head upstairs.

## 12
# Quit

Wouldn't be Saturday without Early being around. If he and Mom aren't busy on Friday evening, and he's not off and away somewhere, then he comes over, and they sip wine and talk. With a friend, once in awhile. Early's had a small number of girlfriends and they've occasionally joined him. Not one of them has ever lasted long. I remember when I was young, Mom had a boyfriend named Robert. I don't know what happened to him. I was too young to remember, too young to be told, probably. She's never included anyone else on Friday nights.

So usually on Saturday mornings, I wake up to the Bug out on the driveway, and Early snoring away in the cot-in-a-corner guestroom. He's family; I like that he's here. But today, after yesterday, and last night – him not knowing what to say to me – I sort of wish he wasn't here. The thought makes me feel ashamed.

Hunger drives me to the kitchen, and there he is standing over the table, forking pancakes onto the three plates he's set out. Saturday routine. I poke around in the fridge, looking for blueberry syrup, and hand it to him, a sort of peace offering. Not that he'd recognize it for that, but I feel a bit better. Mom pads around in her slippers, taking quick sips of coffee, and it's not until I'm settled in with my pancakes, syrup and dollop of cottage cheese — Mom insists on it — that I notice she keeps giving Uncle Early these *looks,* and sighing. Is this about me? And yesterday?

He sets his coffee mug down and she picks it up a minute later and takes it to the sink.

"Whoa, Tessie!" Early says. "I'm not done with the thing yet, sister."

She peers into the mug and there's a slight curl to her lip. "Hhmmph," she says, plunking it down beside him.

"Are you wanting to be rid of me?" Early asks.

"No, of course not," Mom says, but I'm not sure I believe her, and I'm positive Early doesn't, judging by the look on his face. "You're welcome to stay. You always are. You know that. Just thought you might have something better to do."

"You know I don't."

"You would if you'd recognize it for what it was."

Something's going on here that I know nothing about. Mom's mad — steaming mad.

Early's cutting his pancakes and eating faster than I've seen anyone, and when his plate is clean, he marches it to the sink, rinses, plops it in the dishwasher, and starts mopping up the counter. He's mad, too: he only cleans when he's mad. He even goes to the broom closet and rattles around in there. "I keep telling you to get a new mop!" he hollers at Mom from within the closet. "I hate this old thing of yours. It's like chasing a dead bird around the room."

"Use a rag," she says curtly.

"I don't want to clean the floor on my hands and knees."

"A little hands-and-knees would be good for you!" Mom is almost shouting by now.

*Will someone tell me what's going on?*

He backs out of the door, his hands full of fabric, dark green and striped...no, plaid. "Will you look at this?" he blusters. "It's Grand's robe."

"That old thing," says Mom. "It'll do." She hands him the bottle of cleaner and points out the bucket.

"Wait," I say. "I remember that robe. I remember Grand wearing it." I take it from him. The belt is still attached, but one pocket is half torn and droops from the front. It's soft — wool flannel, I think you'd call it — and as I hold it up to my cheek, something washes over me, a sense of...relief. You don't get more real than this plaid flannel robe. I can still remember her padding around in it, tightening the belt, pulling a tissue out of the pocket.

"It was Dad's actually," says Mom now, taking a closer look. "He loved it. She always wore it after he was gone."

Triumph, I feel. *See?* I want to shout. She was as real as you and me. Except yesterday I discovered maybe I'm not so real. Okay, Uncle Early, as real as you.

"I remember it," says Early gruffly, then he moves as if to take it from me.

"Find something else," I say, and I gather it into a bundle and take it up to my room.

When I come back downstairs, he's found a rag and is swatting away at the corners, beside him a bucket full of steaming sudsy water. "Your mom can use some help around here, that's for sure," he says, resting for a moment on his haunches. Is this his way of apologizing to her for whatever she's mad about? Then he's scrubbing away again, and with his back to me, he says, "So, you ready to talk about yesterday? Ready to talk about the jamming out?"

The jamming out. My stomach thuds.

He keeps his back to me, still, and goes on. "It's good to talk about it, Mally girl."

"Are you going to tell me what's between you and Mom?"

His cleaning slows, but he doesn't turn around, and then he's scrubbing even harder, really getting into the corner by the fridge where Mom spilled iced tea a couple of days ago and never got quite to the end of it. "Maybe some things aren't so good to talk about."

"Like what?"

"Like...it's between your mom and me." A sound of impatience, a sort of snort, comes out of him then, and he heaves himself to his feet, drops the rag into the bucket.

"Look, Molly," he says, "maybe it's not for you, girl, the stage and all that life. Maybe there's something else that's yours, and you've yet to find it. You think?"

*No, I don't think. There's only one thing I've ever really wanted.*

"Sometimes things change, you know. They just do. It's how it is."

*Nothing changes for you, Uncle Early, nothing. You always make certain of that.*

He's looking at me oddly, and seems to be waiting for some sort of answer. I don't give him one, and he finishes the floor, but by the time he's finished, I'm back upstairs in my room. I think I hear the front door slam. I assume it's Mom, but moments later she's at my door.

"Where's Early?" she asks, a snap to her voice.

"Early?"

"Yes, my one and only brother. Where'd he go?"

"He must have left."

"Without saying goodbye?"

"I guess so."

She rubs at the top of her head as she does when she's trying not to show me how she feels about something. "Did he say anything to you about yesterday?"

"Not really."

"Not really?"

"Unless you count telling me that maybe it's not for me."

Mom stares at me, and I stare back until she's a blur, then I close my door.

# 13
# Fish-Eye

*M*onday there are no questions and everyone seems to be avoiding what happened. Faces pass in the hall. I feel like a camera with a fish-eye lens: eyes are big and bulging, noses sniff at me, rabbit-like, and mouths curve in big distorted smiles. Everyone's being too nice. It makes it seem so final. Reminds me of Grand's memorial service. But there's a difference: at the service I'd felt so detached from everyone around me, as if there was a space between me and everyone else in the world. No one could step into that space; I remember that feeling, though I can only describe it now that it feels so different. There is no space now. My thoughts swim thickly around me, and there's a closeness, as if I can feel people – people who aren't even touching me – pressing close to me. I don't like it, and I can't get away from it.

And Julian. It's as if he's trying to hunt me down. For

once he looks as if something has affected him. I hear snatches of conversation and I know that he didn't get the role of Max Detweiler after all. Someone else did. But Julian doesn't seem to care at all. He can take it or leave it. He could follow Uncle Early's advice and see if maybe there's something else for him.

His face is everywhere, with that kind, concerned expression. His shadow, Caleb, has that look, too. Some other look, as well, but I'm not sure what that's about. He never says anything to me, not anything at all.

"Julian," I say at last, "tell Ms. Tanaka I can't make it to class today. I don't feel well."

He frowns at my words. Then clears his throat. "Is that it?" he asks. "You're just going to give up?"

I can't help but notice Caleb shoving his elbow into Julian's ribs. Julian frowns harder. "Whatever then," he says and turns away.

I spend the next block in the homework hall, trying to focus on French.

Wednesday. I walk slowly to class. The bell has sounded, the hall is empty, and I can hear the usual sounds of drama class, how it must always sound from the outside. I move closer to the door, and on the door is a piece of paper. The cast of *The Sound of Music*. Already the paper is soft at the edges, tape unstuck at one corner. It's not needed now: every name on that list belongs to someone who can't possibly forget what's on it.

I hear a murmur that is Ms. Tanaka's, and a high-pitched laugh – Katherine's. The whole class is suddenly roaring. Now would be a good time to slip in. The longer I put it off, the harder it's going to be; that's what I tell myself over and over. It's just drama class. Like math class or P.E. Nothing more.

I put my hand to the knob. There's a sudden draft in the hallway and under my hand the knob trembles. Think about how Julian breezes into class. Easy...have a blast...I try not to see Julian's Monday frown, and I ignore the drooping list on the door and turn the knob.

The door is open. Most of the students are turned away, but Ms. Tanaka turns toward me and opens her mouth to speak. I think my face stops her. *Don't say anything to me. Pretend I'm not here.*

I stay near the door for the rest of class as much as possible. During improv-tag no one touches me, and I avoid Ms. Tanaka's eyes, and I look to the clock on the wall again and again, until it is time to leave. The end of the day. I pretend not to notice Julian following me out after class to where Candace waits by the maple.

She smiles at me, but speaks to Julian. "So," she says, "did you drag Molly into class?"

*Hello? I'm right here in front of you,* I want to shout.

"She came, all on her own." He speaks with a big smile as if he's a parent and I just took my first steps.

"Good," says Candace. "I was starting to think she wasn't

going to after last Friday."

I interrupt this. "Can we talk about something else? And maybe talk *to* me!" I wish I had a sitcom scriptwriter sitting in my head, someone to come up with some funny talk. But Candace continues to speak to Julian. "Did she hang out at the back of the class?"

How well she knows me!

"Or did she get into it and do whatever it is you guys do?"

That's when Julian misses a beat. After a pause – brief but still a pause – he says: "It's sort of difficult to hide out in a drama class."

He doesn't say that I tried my best, though.

I can hear Mom's voice in my head: *They're concerned for you.*

"You're going to be fine," says Candace, finally speaking to me.

"You sound like my mom," I say.

"Well, you will be," she says. "It can't happen twice."

"They used to say that about lightning, and now they know better."

Candace turns onto the sidewalk and begins to walk home. "Remember when I spent two months carving that giraffe? Then I used a new chisel and the whole thing split?"

"It's not the same. That didn't happen in front of a kazillion people."

Now there's an odd expression on Candace's face. "You're right," she says. "I guess that's the difference between performing arts and other arts."

"Maybe you take this too seriously," Julian says to me. "It should be fun – the show must go on!"

"*You* don't take *anything* seriously," I say.

"Sure I do. Some things," he says. Then he gives Candace this LOOK, and it's as if someone rips the blindfold from my eyes. I can't believe I didn't see it before. Julian likes Candace.

I'm so stunned I stop walking, and the two of them keep on, matching stride for stride, like the walking-on-the-beach scene in a movie. At first they don't even notice I'm not there, and by the time they do, I wish I wasn't anywhere near them. Candace looks back. "Coming?" she says.

I mumble about forgetting something, and turn and walk away. Why does it bother me so much, this discovery about Julian and Candace? I like Julian, but it's not as if I was scribbling M.G. + J.S. in the margins of my notebooks. *Molly Smart*. No, nothing like that! I'd just thought he was cute. Nice. I thought maybe he liked me.

But there's a voice in me: *come on, Molly. You knew! You knew it was Candace all the time!* And another voice: *if this had happened a week ago, would it bother you as much as it does now?* Where are these voices coming from lately?

The voices are almost shut down by the sound of the door closing behind me after I enter the school. At least I no longer feel Candace and Julian's eyes in my back. I start down the hallway, and wonder where I should go. It doesn't matter, really, just away somewhere. The halls turn and I follow. There are still corners I've not found in the past three weeks, it seems. I follow a few turns and find myself outside the front door of the theatre. I start to turn away, but hear a voice.

"Molly!" It's Ms. Tanaka. "Come in!" She seems so pleased to see me. "We could use an extra set of hands here." She's holding the door wide open.

I hesitate. A thought passes through my mind of what's outside: Candace and Julian, though probably long gone now. And I step into the cavernous auditorium. It's a different place to what it was audition day. There's the low hum of work taking place.

"There's a meeting about graduation, and too many of my folks haven't shown up," says Ms. Tanaka. "I could use your help – you can be the stage manager." She hands me a board with a sheaf of papers clipped to it, and I see that it's the script. Before I know it, a pencil is in my hand, and I'm taking notes, sitting up centre-front.

The von Trapp "children" are in a line upstage, and Ms. Tanaka works through their steps. "This way, Louisa...crossing paths with Brigitta...where's Brigitta? I'm sure I saw her here just a moment ago. How can I block with no one here?" Her words are grumpy but her face and her tone of voice are not. She has her sleeves rolled up and her hair is tied back. She's ready to work. "There she is, my Brigitta." The student comes through the door and hurries into position. "Now for Marta..."

I'm scribbling on the page, marking where Brigitta is, and should be, and how she's supposed to move.

"How are those notes coming, Molly?" Ms. Tanaka asks from on stage. "Are you getting it all? Marta and Gretl need to be here when *So Long* begins."

I mark in Gretl's place. "I'm getting it," I say.

Ms. Tanaka surveys the stage and my eyes follow hers. Three guys from art class are painting blue and lavender alps in the far corner. A guy and a girl from carpentry are joining two pieces of set with hinges and arguing. Ms. Tanaka flaps a hand at them as if to say, Get over it.

"What about you?" she says, turning suddenly to me. "You can stand in for Marta for now. I can't block without someone being here. Come, and bring the board with you."

I go to the stairs. *I'm just standing in*, I tell myself. Ms. Tanaka moves around, pushes us into place, stands back to see how it looks. The girl playing Brigitta grins at me, at what I'm not sure: maybe just at the sight of Ms. Tanaka bustling, and at the beehive action in general.

"Marta has a line here, Molly," calls out Ms. Tanaka.

I start, and look at the papers in my hands. "Right..." It must be the page under this. I push it away, and look for the name MARTA on the next. When I look up, Ms. Tanaka is looking at me, and I look past her, to the rows of chairs backing into the darkness.

I'm up here, aren't I? Somehow, my feet counted up those stairs, and here I am. I look down, try to focus, but the words on the page blur, and I hug the clipboard to me, my arms cold. It's happening again, I can feel it.

The art guys are pulling a piece of alps out onto the stage, and I have to make my way around them. They don't look at me as I pass. I don't think anyone does, really, and I should feel grateful for that, but I can feel the teacher's eyes on me as I hit the bottom stair.

"Molly?" she whispers.

I just shake my head, and head out, out to where I left Candace and Julian, out down the sidewalk home. Out.

Home, and Mom hears me come in, and she knows something is wrong, but she says nothing, just follows me to my room, then hangs back as I close my door behind me.

*Don't ask. Just don't ask. Just leave me alone.*

That's what Greta Garbo said, wasn't it? The Great Garbo, beloved by the Great Grand. No wonder Mom was angry when I said she was jealous of Grand. Jealous of Grand! Why, there was nothing to be jealous of! *We were a couple of fakes, Grand and me. Except Grand got to pretend all her life, and for me it's over now, age fourteen. Done. I know I'm not an actress, never was. The stage does not belong to me, to Grand. Never did.*

I yank open the closet door, and go after the boxes. Pull off the lids, and move from one wall to the next. Garbo's the first down, and as I throw the second into the box, I can hear glass breaking. A few nails pop out of the wall and clatter to the floor. In two minutes, every picture is off my walls, all those glossy faces, Olivier and Vivian Leigh and even that silly Mortimer Snerd.

I'm amazed that I don't hear Mom at the door wondering what on earth...

I turn off the lights and crawl into bed, pull the quilt up. But even with it over my head, I can still see those empty walls. *Sorry, Grand, sorry. I thought I had it in me. But I don't.*

I don't.

## 14
# G is for Goatherd

The bell rings, signalling drama class. Hallways are empty. I'm not deliberately late. It's just that my feet seem slow to move. My hand is on the knob. I hear a laugh from Julian.

I can't do this.

Early's words have been on my mind all week. Now I hear them again, in his voice: *just quit.*

The exit door is only twenty feet away. It squeaks as I open it. If anyone hears, they're choosing not to do anything about it. I know what'll happen though: the phone call from the secretary, the questions from Mom.

But that doesn't happen. Instead, Monday morning, there's a note for me in homeroom. It's from Ms. Tanaka.

*Molly, I'd like to speak with you today. At lunchtime, if you can. I've missed you.*

*Ms. Tanaka.*

I've let her down, haven't I?

I fold the note and put it in my pocket. At noon I find her waiting for me. In the drama room, she has a corner with bookshelves of plays and monologues and two couches. She sits on one and motions me to the other. She starts. "I've been wondering what we can do about this."

Then we sit, looking at each other, neither of us with an answer.

"Mr. Roman led me to believe that you are very serious about wanting to act and to be on stage..."

Again, I say nothing. I feel as if I can't say anything, really. Even if I wanted to.

Ms. Tanaka sighs, a heavy adult sigh. She looks as if she's considering whether to not to speak. Finally: "How about a non-speaking role?" she asks.

*Kinda like this?* I think, still trying to will words to my mouth.

She shakes her head. Then she says: "What about...the puppet scene? With the goatherd and the girl? I have a couple of marionettes, and I need someone..." Her voice drifts as she sees my face.

"Molly?" Ms. Tanaka's head is cocked.

"Puppets," I say numbly. "It's okay, I..."

"Look," she says, and goes to the props cupboard. She pulls out a brightly striped box. "I found these when I was in Austria years ago." Out comes a boy puppet, in lederhosen and a peaked hat.

Her eyes are bright as she holds out the puppet to me. "It works like this. This controls the feet, and this the hands." In her hands, the puppet dances, legs crossing like scissors, feet flying, arms in the air overhead.

I don't want anything more to do with this. I don't want to hear the word 'stage.' I don't want to think 'out there.' I don't want to hear about puppets. I am done. *I am done.*

The thought excites me in a terrible way. As if it's all up to me, and I can walk away from it. I can be done with it. I see it all leading to this: tearing down Grand's pictures, skipping class. Yes, I can be free. The very thought pushes me to my feet. I stand to go.

"Not for me," I say.

"I was hoping..." Ms. Tanaka begins.

"I know. Thanks," I say.

I make it to the door before she speaks again.

"Molly!"

I don't want to turn around and look at her.

"I do know what it's like to have something come between you and your dreams," she says softly.

I nod. Yeah, sure. Ms. Tanaka has been in New York, on stage.

I can't speak. I close the door behind me.

Candace wraps up what's left of her lunch and then pulls out a small bag of almonds. "Where were you?"

"I had a note from Ms. Tanaka. She tried to talk me into being a puppeteer, doing the lonely goatherd routine."

Candace begins to yodel.

"Yeah, Ms. T. would probably like to teach me how to do that, too...will you stop?"

She does. "You said no?"

"I said no. I said not for me!"

Candace thinks about that for a moment.

"Might be fun though," she ventures, and appears to be about to start yodeling again.

"Don't! Please! And I think it would be about as much fun as that old art class of yours."

Candace shudders. "No, nothing could be that bad. The potato printing was like eating spinach, and making paper lanterns was like eating liver. What a choice: A Lot of Yuck or A Lot More Yuck. Now it's guitar, and everyone in the class is way ahead of me. Makes me want to go to my room with no dinner!"

"Well, at least you have Julian. What's he? Chocolate cake, or Häagen-Dazs ice cream?" *Wow. Can't believe I just said that. Now it's out.*

She looks at me, amazed, mouth hanging open. Then snaps it shut. "Oh," she says wretchedly, "he does like me, doesn't he?"

My turn to be surprised. "What's wrong with that?"

She shakes her head. "I don't want a boyfriend. Yet," she adds.

"Well, I've heard there's a fine goatherd..."

Candace throws an almond at me. "Shut up!" she says.


I unlock the front door, throw my jacket over a chair and open the fridge for milk, pour it, and sit.

Then I hear it: a moan. My neck prickles. It takes a half minute to set the glass of milk back on the table without making a sound, and prepare to run.

Another moan, and with it, another thought. Maybe someone has broken into the house and tied up Mom.

The sound is low and ragged. That would be the duct tape they've gagged her with. Then the next thought: they might still be in the house.

I taste blood and realize I'm biting my lip. I reach into the cutlery drawer. Why is it wide open? Was Mom going to reach for a knife, too? The bone handle of Mom's ancient bread knife is in my grasp, and I move to the entrance hall, and the Hole, where the sound is coming from. I picture Mom in there amongst all that old storage junk. Then stop.

What if the intruder's still upstairs? It couldn't take more than five minutes to discover there's nothing valuable in this house. Which means he'll be right back down here. I should grab the phone and dash into the front yard, screaming for help. But what about Mom?

Another moan. And another. Maybe he's still in there. I clench the knife, hold it high, and tiptoe across the living room to the door in the hallway. It's open just a crack — I push gently.

There's Mom all right. "Oh, Molly," she says, in this strangely hushed voice, and she turns absolutely red. She's not tied up, I see. She's holding something she doesn't have a chance of hiding: a cello, I think it is. I've never seen one up close. She must be holding the bow behind her back. "It sounds awful, doesn't it?" she says.

"I thought a burglar had hurt you and thrown you in here."

She looks astonished. "*That* bad? Really?" She starts to laugh. I nod, and her face gets redder and redder, but her eyes are all lit up and she laughs until tears come from the corners and run down her cheeks.

"A burglar, Mom, a BURGLAR!"

She laughs harder.

"I'm serious," I say. "I was scared!" Is she going to be the second person today to tell me I'm too serious?

She hugs the neck of the cello to her, and drops her head so I can't see her face, just her shoulders shaking. The cello supports her — good thing, because she's getting wobbly with all that mirth. I almost feel like yanking it away from her. It's not *that* funny, is it?

Mom sets the bow to the strings, and the poor thing moans again. "You try it," she says, and I feel the gentle prod of the bow just above my hip. She's holding it out to me. "Come on – can't be any worse."

But my sounds are much worse: a screech that makes my teeth buzz, and I push the bow back to her. "Where on earth did you get this thing? You didn't pay for it, did you?"

"Of course not!" She pats the golden-stained wood. "It was in Grand's storage locker at the home. They've been holding it since April. They called me last week to come and clean it out, and I was just putting it away in here, and thought I'd open the case."

"I don't remember Grand ever playing the cello."

Mom runs her finger down a string. "I don't think this has ever been played." She sets it into the case, and wheels it through a narrow path she's made, into a corner. "Maybe it was another Grand dream. I thought I'd try to sell it, and realized I know even less about selling it than I do about playing it."

"So you're going to play this thing?"

"Why not?" she says wonderingly. Then she turns to me. "What would you think if I had spent money on it?"

What would I think? Maybe that hadn't been the right question for her to ask.

She doesn't wait for my answer. "It's been a long time since I spent money on something for me. It wouldn't hurt."

"But would you really hide out to practice in the Hole?" I ask.

She looks around the little space, at the shelves covered in old skates, shoes, boots, badminton racquets, magazines. "I was thinking of turning this storage space into a library. Somewhere for my books, and to practise." She motions to the wall. "Cut in a window even...A window seat." Her voice drifts off. "Oh, maybe not."

## 15

# Turkey's Out

*A*ll day there's been an odd-looking object on the counter, hiding under a wet towel. Mom catches me looking at it, and she sounds rather irritated when she tells me what it is. "A turkey. And don't tell me you didn't know."

"A turkey?"

"For Thanksgiving," she explains.

"Why's it all shrunken like that?"

"It's a small one," she says. "I wasn't sure what we were going to do for Thanksgiving this year."

"What we always do!"

But her face puckers.

"It's their turn here – Avery and Candace. Last year it was at their house, remember?"

Still Mom hesitates.

"Or," I say, "we could just forget the whole thing. I'm not

feeling very thankful lately anyway!"

Mom chooses to ignore that. "It's just...I haven't heard from Avery."

"What's there to hear – who does the broccoli?" I decide to get to the point, as I see it. "And what about Uncle Early?"

Mom sighs. "Then there's *that.*

There is *that,* isn't there.

Uncle Early has his Thanksgiving tasks. The roast beast is his job. He makes a big fuss and grumbles, but won't let anyone help him until the big melee at the end, the coming together of carving and gravy-making and getting the potatoes and yams right. I wonder what he's going to do about it this year?

"Have you heard from Uncle Early?"

Mom looks under the towel and pokes at the bird as if it's her brother. "I've left him messages," she says, and she doesn't sound hopeful.

I can't believe he's gone away and not let us know where he is or anything at all. He's always kept in touch when he goes away. I have to ask: "Are you two still fighting?"

She frowns, which means she doesn't want to answer.

"Mom, he never misses a holiday."

"He does seem to be planning otherwise this time." She seems so sad, that I feel a splat of anger toward my uncle. Can't he work this out, whatever it is, with Mom?

"Well, we don't need him!" I give the turkey a poke, too. Then take another look under the towel. "There's not enough here for him, anyway. This poor turkey looks as if it was a long-distance runner bird."

"Just before the run of his life," says Mom. But she sounds as if only half her thoughts are with me.

"I'll call Candace. *We'll* work it out." But with my cooking ability, I sound more confident than I am.

The next day, Avery's not feeling too well, so we decide to pack up the turkey and roast it at their house. Still no word from Early, so it'll be us four. Mom pours the pumpkin pie filling into a juice jug, snaps on a tight lid, and we set off.

Candace is nowhere in sight when we arrive. Mom begins to pull everything out and set it on the counter. She's cut the onions and celery at home, and now the room fills with the smell of browning butter, sage and pepper. Avery sits in a wicker rocking chair, with her feet on a stool. She's had the sniffles for days and is just tired, she says. I can see it's not easy for her to sit and watch Mom.

"Candace has been in her room since Friday," says Avery, with a look toward the laundry room door. "She occasionally comes out for food."

"Maybe the smell will lure her," says Mom with a grin. "In the meantime, you start the chain, Molly."

"Do we have to do the chain this year?" I ask. I can't think of anything to be thankful for.

"I'll start," says Avery, glad for something to do. I hand her a few strips of the coloured paper Mom packed without me noticing – she's good at that sort of thing – and a coloured pen. But after I hand it to her, Avery doesn't do anything with it, except sit there and stare at the bright strips.

"Every year we do this," she says. "We write out what we're thankful for and attach all the pieces into a paper chain and decorate. Remember the year it went all the way around the kitchen?"

"I remember," Mom says.

I remember, too. Last year, we sat around the table at our house – six of us with Grand – and we'd laughed as we put words on paper. Even last year, the chain had looped around the wall behind the table and over the doorway. There'd been a lot to be thankful for. I never thought I'd be feeling thankful just for the easy laughter we'd had then at the table. This year, everything seems so much more complicated.

"I'm having a hard time coming up with something," Avery says, fingering the paper. Finally she begins to roll it, absentmindedly, into a small and smaller tube.

I pick up a pen, too, but my mind's completely blank.

Mom looks up from peeling potatoes. "You two!" she scolds. "If that's all you're gonna do, *you* can peel these stupid potatoes, and *I'll* write something." She plunks the potatoes and peeler on the counter and pulls up a chair, wiping her hands on a towel. "Let's see..." she begins, but it doesn't take her long, and she's writing on a golden strip. *I am thankful for good friends.* Then she starts on another.

Avery rests her chin on her hands and thinks. Then she sighs, a big breath, and sort of shudders. Mom looks at her sharply. "The baby's healthy – that's something," she says.

"Yes," Avery agrees, "that is something." She writes it down dutifully. Then goes back to resting her chin on her hands and staring at Mom, as if it's up to Mom to come up with something else. "I don't suppose you've heard from Early, have you?" she asks softly. Mom looks up from her writing.

"No, I haven't." They sit there, looking at each other, before Mom gets very busy writing on another strip of paper. Avery watches her for a moment before picking up a second strip. She begins to write something, then scribbles it out, crumples the paper. "You know," she says, "I'm just not sure I want to do this, this year."

And while all this is happening, or not happening, depending on how you look at it, a feeling is beginning to crawl over me. *Avery…and Early. Early and Avery.* Why didn't I see it before?

Mom is calmly filling out a third or fourth paper strip, and she's begun to join them together. And she's so *normal* looking. She looks up and catches my eyes, and her face flushes a sudden pink, and that's my confirmation. The crawly feeling quickens, and covers me. I look back at Avery, and I don't see my friend's mother, the woman I usually see, the woman who loves to sew and create colourful things, who laughs and frequently has a quick and funny story. Instead I see a tired, sick-with-a-cold woman almost six and a half months pregnant – she looks huge to me! – and she's by herself, and she's just a bit scared. Maybe a whole lot scared.

If Early were here, I think I'd whack him on the side of the head. Or beg him to tell me it's not what I think, it's not.

Mom says, "Molly, why don't you go see what Candace is up to?"

"I'll do that," I say. "I'll, uh, take up some of these paper strips." *And I'm going to write on one just how thankful I am that I can escape this half of the house, the Avery half.* I reach the top of the stairs outside Candace's room, though, and have to brush a cobweb from my hair. This is the Candace half of their world. I push open the door, and I'm glad Candace has finally cleared the stacks of books from the window, and end-of-afternoon light is coming through. She's put a large piece of styrofoam on the wall beside the workbench, and with long pins has skewered buttons to it in stripes of colour. The various hues of each colour, all grouped, has created a magical and shimmering effect. "Wow," I say.

She smiles. "Collage," she says, "is a great distraction."

"From being thankful? From spiders' webs?"

"From almost anything." She pushes the next pin so hard that the button sinks into the foam and she has to use a crochet hook to lift it back into place. I don't say what I'm thinking: that it's not the collage that's the distraction, but the thrusting of the pins. Candace's voodoo!

"What are you grinning about?" she asks, but she's grinning, too.

"Can I put a few on?"

She hands me some pins. "You can start at the other end, with the light buttons." She motions to the pile of buttons, and she notices the paper strips. "You're doing the Thanks Chain again, aren't you?"

"Mom says. You know how it is."

Candace skewers in another piece of red plastic. "I can't think of anything to be thankful for."

The word 'Julian' floats into my mind. *How about that, Candace?* My own pin goes deeply into the foam. "Where's that crochet hook?" I ask.

"How grumpy are you about this turkey thing?"

"I can handle turkey." That's the least of it. She works on her end, and I on mine. But the turkey dinner has always been dependent on those strips of paper. No paper, no turkey. It's kind of scary to poke around inside myself and not find anything to be grateful for. Finally, I write,

*Candace talks to me now.*

She picks it up and reads. "Don't let my mom see that one."

"I can't imagine not talking with my mom."

"We *talk*. It's just that she doesn't say anything important."

"That's like not talking."

Candace fingers the paper. "Maybe I'll skip the turkey this year. I'll become vegetarian!"

"You know what my mom would say: no thanks, no veggies."

"At least you have your mom to yourself." She puts the pen to the paper as if that'll help.

"I've always shared Mom with Uncle Early," I say.

Candace looks up quickly. "Where *is* your uncle?"

I shrug. There's that horrible crawly feeling again; how can I know what I think I know, and keep it from my best friend?

"Where do you think he's gone?" she asks again.

"No idea." I'm not sure I trust myself to say more, and I pick up some things from her worktable: a cigar, or at least the end of a cigar, and a shriveled bit of balloon that she stretches out for me. The words on the yellow rubber read 'It's a Boy!'

"I found them by the side of the road," Candace says. "They must have fallen out of someone's car. What do you think?"

"What are they for — I mean, what are *you* going to use them for?"

"My next collage, a collage of fathers. I think I'm gonna call it *Don't Wannabees*. Maybe you have a contribution?"

Does she suspect I know something? I'd like just to tell her. We're friends; friends share secrets. It's the nature of friendship, and the nature of secrets. "My father," I begin — the phrase feels rusty — "was cruising down the fast lane minding his own business on his motorbike. It's not that he didn't want to be."

"I'm sorry," says Candace. "I didn't mean your father."

*What* did *you mean?* Candace has begun to write. *I'm thankful for chisels and wood.* And on another strip: *I'm thankful for buttons and foam.*

*I'm thankful for a change of subject.* But I don't write that on a strip of paper. Between us we add three links to Mom's half dozen and Avery's one.

## 16

# Disconnected

Outside, the October wind is cold and tears through my jersey shirt. I set off down the sidewalk, but hear a honk of a horn.

Mom. "I was going to grab a few groceries and come and pick you up. But this is better. I need you to come downtown with me to Early's place."

I climb in and expect her to ask me why I'm leaving school an hour early, but she doesn't. "Are you all right?" I ask.

"No," she says shortly.

"He still hasn't answered your calls?"

"Worse," she says. "His phone's disconnected."

She pulls away from the curb, and I take a deep breath. "Does this have anything to do with...Avery?" I whisper the name.

Then Mom takes a breath. For a minute I think — hope — that she's going to say no. Then she says yes. She doesn't even ask me how I guessed. "You really shouldn't say anything to Candace. You and I aren't supposed to know. Avery and Early have decided not to tell anyone."

I feel a surge of anger. Are adults so stupid?

"I don't understand it myself," Mom says. "It seems ostrich-like, poking your head in the sand and thinking that if you can't see it, it must not be there. Easier for Early, I'd think. It's hard to ignore a belly the size of Avery's!"

When she says that though, all I can see is my uncle's face, and how miserable he's looked lately. "He'll let us know where he is," I say. But will he, or is this it? The time that Mom's always expected? The time he just goes. I remember that when I was young and he was setting off on one of his trips, I would ask him where he was going this time, and the answer was always the same: "No place in particular, Mally-girl." It always stuck in my mind as the city of No Place, in the country of Particular. It wasn't until I was years older that I realized he was travelling for work, for taking photos, and knew exactly where he was going. Now I wonder: Do they have phones in No Place? If Early had a cell phone, like a normal person, well, it wouldn't even matter where in Particular he was — we could reach him.

We speed downtown, to the east side, Early's place. FOR RENT reads the black and orange sign in his attic window. His landlord is washing the window, barely keeping his balance clutching the fire escape ladder.

"It's probably not the best time to speak with him," I begin, but Mom's way ahead of me.

"Where's Early?" Her voice is shrill.

"Moved," is the answer. He's not the least bit startled by her calling out.

"Moved?"

"Yeah. Gone. I'm gonna miss him. Nine years is a long time."

"When did he leave?"

"Must be almost two weeks now. Sudden decision, he said. Couldn't give notice. Offered to pay, though. I said forget it."

"That was nice of you," says Mom automatically. "Do you know where he went?"

"Nope. Figure he's travelling far this time."

Mom makes a funny sound, more than taking in a breath this time. Maybe taking in a breath with a big old blue-bottle fly or something.

"Say!" Recognition dawns in the eyes of the landlord. "You're his sister, aren't you?"

"Yes."

"He left something for you. Said you'd come around." The man clambers down from his perch, and disappears into the house. We wait, and he reappears. "Better come with me. Too big to bring out." He peers around us to see the car. "Don't know if it'll fit in *that*."

"He didn't leave us that ghastly couch, did he?" asks Mom.

The man laughs. "Nope. That's for me. Means I can rent the place as 'furnished.'"

"He didn't take his furniture?"

"Said he wouldn't need it where he's going."

"Did he take his suitcases?"

"Yep. Packed full."

We follow him into the dark basement, and when he flicks on a light, we can see all of Early's paintings neatly stacked against the walls with what is probably his entire collection of bath and dish towels tucked between them to prevent scratching.

"His art collection?" Mom stands absolutely still.

"Sculpture, too." He motions to the enormous tortoise in the corner. Papier mâché – wait till Candace sees this.

"Where are we going to put all this?" When Mom is angry, her voice is nothing like Early's. It's loud. "It's one thing to take care of my brother and quite another to have to take care of his art collection!"

"He mentioned you'd say something like that." The man chuckles. "He said to tell you one's as important as the other."

Mom sniffs, and picks up a canvas in each hand. "Molly, open the trunk please, and we'll stuff these in."

Grumpy as she sounds, she does not stuff them in, and it takes an hour to arrange the collection in the car. The landlord follows with the last load. "I'm gonna miss your brother. I'm missing our morning coffees already, and putting our feet up in the middle of his mess. Amazing how he could relax in the middle of chaos." He chuckles.

"He didn't leave you with a disaster, did he?" Mom asks.

Another laugh. "No, no, he wouldn't do that. You know that. I think he shovelled everything into a corner and stuffed it in a bag."

"We'll take the bag," I say quickly.

Mom looks astonished.

"It'll fit on top of the art."

"I'll have no rear vision," she protests.

I've already set off for the top floor of the house. I admit I almost expect to see Early there, or at least *feel* him, but no, there's only an emptiness. And a very large garbage bag.

"You don't need to do this," says the landlord.

"I do." I hoist the bag over a shoulder. Paper rustles inside. A clue, perhaps. I say nothing of my hopes to Mom as I take my seat in front, and share it with a naked sandstone woman in my lap. It's hard to know how or where to hold her.

"No address. No phone number," Mom keeps muttering, threading through traffic. "No note. Nothing." Voice getting loud, louder.

"Mom, he'll let us know where he is. He's okay. We'll get a postcard."

Mom wallops the steering wheel with her hand. "A

postcard!? To tell us he's okay. Having a good time! But what about the people he's left behind?"

I say nothing. It's better that way.

At home, before we can make dinner, we empty the car. "It'll all have to go in the Hole. It's the only place big enough," says Mom finally. I can tell she's reluctant to give up her library, her cello practice room. "I'm glad I didn't take the doors off yet," she says. I'm surprised to see how much she's cleared out already. And now, we're quickly filling it again.

"We could hang some on the walls," I suggest, and Mom stops, mid-motion, and stands there holding a canvas to herself.

"There's an idea." She sets down the one she's carrying, and begins to flip through those we've put in the Hole. "This one!" she says. "I've always loved this one." She looks for a hook. "Where should we put it? I won't have my library, but I'll settle for a gallery."

"Why don't we put it in your room?"

"My room?"

Why is she so surprised? She should have thought of it herself. "Yeah, your room."

Mom's done that light-coloured walls, optical illusion thing in her room, to try to make it look bigger. She's replaced the double bed I remember from when I was a kid with a single, and her desk takes up most of the space, her file cabinet the rest. This is where she works as well as sleeps. She must dream in numbers.

"I think you need a piece of art in there," I say. The walls are bare. There's not even a photo of my father, which, come to think of it, is sort of weird. There are photographs of him elsewhere in the house. Why not her room?

Mom stands, hands on hips. "I do need a piece of art, Mol o'mine." She's nodding.

Five minutes later we stand, looking at the Eiffel Tower, a painting of great slashes of black and so much cobalt blue.

"Did you ever want to go to Paris?"

"I'm not dead, Molly!" she says, with a laugh. "I might get there yet."

I push the bulging bag of garbage under my bed, glad Mom seems to have forgotten about it for the time being. When she's asleep I'll open it.

# 17
# Let's Make a Deal

*H*ow can I get out of drama class? There's Candace, in guitar and learning to strum. Can I skip more? Mom said nothing about the inevitable phone call from the secretary. In the second semester, I'll have a free block. Maybe I can just quit drama now and take something else then.

But of course when I ask the counsellor, she gives me a funny look instead of an answer.

"Maybe I could quit and take summer school, then?"

"You could do that," she says with reluctance. "But it seems like a lot of work. Some kids sign up for drama for fun, easy credits. It's not biology or history, you know."

Fun and Easy. Try Tough and Terrifying. Why dissect a frog when you can do it to yourself? *Yoo hoo! Here's my spleen now!*

"Is there an opening in a biology class?"

"We're halfway through October," she says. "It's too late."
I knew that.

"Talk with Ms. Tanaka about her requirements. It would be a shame to fail." The counsellor's voice is kind enough, but she shuffles papers on her desk, jots a note to herself as some thought comes into her head, and pours herself coffee from a Thermos. My problem is not worthy of full attention.

But it's now the end of the week, and I don't even pause outside the door of the drama class. I'll leave through the exit door closest to the French class.

When I hear Ms. Tanaka's voice, I jump. My books crash to the ground. I'm glad for that: she can't see my face while I'm bent over.

"Sorry to startle you."

"Aren't you supposed to be teaching?"

"Aren't you supposed to be in class?"

I wince.

"Mr. Edward's filling in for me," she says.

"Doesn't he teach phys. ed.?"

She shrugs. It's Friday and she's wearing jeans. "Sometimes I feel as if I teach phys. ed." She looks tired suddenly. "Look." She faces me abruptly. "I'll make you a deal: come to class once a week, take your place in the December variety show, and I'll give you a passing grade. Take it or leave it."

"If I leave it?"

"I'll have no choice but to fail you. And failing kids puts me in therapy."

"How long do I have to decide?"

She looks at her watch and leans against the wall. "One minute," she says, timing, "starting now!"

'Forget it' is my first impulse. Then I have an image of the summer, hanging out at the beach...with homework.

Impulse number two: I could sing "Somewhere Over the Rainbow." I've done that before. Though that doesn't guarantee anything, does it?

"Can I lip-synch?" I ask with a half grin. I don't expect her to answer.

"Yes." Her answer is quick. Something fishy here. She's back to checking her watch.

"What else?" I demand.

She shakes her head. "That's it. Really. Lip-synch a Christmas song. A tune the audience will sing with you, if you want! Sleep your way through class once a week, and that's it. No summer school. No big ugly F on your report card. Deal?"

Still I pause. "Can I wear a mask?"

"Wear a paper bag, for all I care!" She sounds impatient. *Think of the summer – free!* "Okay, I'll do it."

Even as I say the words my stomach starts to squeeze, from the very bottom, up into my lungs. Where's that gust of wind when you need some air? Ms. Tanaka doesn't seem to notice anything wrong. She's already marching away to reclaim her class.

"See you next week then," she calls over her shoulder.

I watch after her, unable to speak. I'd run after her but my legs are mushy. *What have I done?* I have to wait for a moment before I can make my way to the door.

I know Early had papers all over his apartment, but it's overwhelming to actually look at each piece. This must be what it's like to be one of those celebrity-garbage people, though at least I don't have to wipe off wet coffee grounds and porridge smears. Wait. Celebrities don't have to eat porridge, do they? My mind wanders as I wade through the pile, and I try to keep it on task. Along with all the full-size pages, there are fragments, ripped corners with a word or two on them, and a hole from a pin. He must have had these tacked all over his bulletin board. What's with the grocery lists? *Bananas. Extension cord.* Who writes that on a piece of paper and keeps it? The recycling bag is growing fat. This piece has nothing on it. I toss it. No, wait. In faint pencil. The lead must have broken, because it's just an impression on paper: *No Place*, followed by a dot and a letter c and a torn edge.

*No Place.* In Particular. Quit pulling my leg.

*You're a big pain, Uncle Early, you know that? A big grown-up pain.* Thursday at lunch.

"Coming to drama class tomorrow?" Julian asks.

"I have to." I grimace.

Julian looks quizzical, but I'm not going to tell him about the deal.

"Tomorrow's costume and character day," he goes on. "Gotta wear a costume. It'll be a blast."

*What isn't, for you?*

"What are you wearing?" Candace asks him.

His grin is just a little coy. "Can't tell you. You'll have to guess! Might be tricky." He leans close to Candace. "Might even be so disguised, you won't know who I am."

Sounds like time for me to bring on the paper bag.

## 18
# The Beggar and Santa Claus

T he old dress-up trunk is now in the spare room, under a box of mitts, gloves and scarves. Everything in the trunk smells forgotten and unwanted. Velvet vests, pirate and cowboy scarves, a black cape that could turn you into Dracula, a wizard, a witch. Wigs I remember buying from rummage sales. My old favourite: a hairpiece from the 1960s, shiny and jelly-bean red. I pull on a wig of long black, tousled hair. I used to put it on and dance like the kids in the Peanuts gang. Mom and Early would laugh, Early until he had tears coming out of his eyes. And I'd dance faster and faster until the wig fell off. No matter what, it always cheered them, me in that wig.

Now I look at myself in the hallway mirror. I can hardly see my face, just two eyes peering through. Makes me think of Ben Gunn, the marooned character in *Treasure Island,* his hair all grown out after years of no haircuts, his eyes restless and just a little crazy.

I dig out the brown blanket I know is in the trunk, so worn, full of holes, and a pair of thigh-high suede boots, Mom's from when she was young. I take it all to my room. I'll be a medieval beggar, a creature to be left alone.

I'll try out the character on Mom. But when I knock on her door I discover she's not there. The lights are off, and the screen saver is travelling on her computer, a Christmas photo of all of us: Mom, Early, Grand, me, Candace, and Avery.

I pull the wig off my head — it's a sweaty old thing — and throw the cape-blanket onto Mom's bed. I sit at Mom's computer.

SEARCH. Where? *Early, Early, Early. O Uncle, where art thou, miserable uncle.*

I type in NO PLACE. Yeah, right. But a page full of possibilities comes up. Some guy's poetry — morose with a capital M. And the guy asks for feedback. I type in "Eeyore, give up eating thistles for breakfast, try some honey." Uncle Early has company, I see.

Back to possibilities. Towards the bottom of the screen, I read No Place In Particular Retreat, Montana State. I click, and on screen looms a photo of a string of cabins by water. *Can't be. Can't be this easy. But of course: No Place dot com.*

There's an email address on the site. I write: "You have a

guest named Early Hyland. Tell him to call home." I can hear Mom's steps on the stairs. Back to the screen saver, and everybody still grinning away.

In the morning I stuff a bag with the wig, the blanket, and the boots into my locker until drama class. I like the idea of going to class covered head to toe. I've also brought some long leather boot laces and brown makeup.

Five minutes before drama class I'm in the ancient change room down the hall from the classroom. It's almost never used, and quite dim. The janitors must forget to renew the light bulbs here. I pull on the boots. One of the heels has a deep crack, and it makes a sad, broken sound as I cross the tile floor. I bind each leg, criss-crossing the leather laces, and feel suddenly that perhaps I once did live long ago, in a place of stone buildings with thatched roofs, in a time of fires for cooking, a time when people actually used the word 'whence.'

The wig I fasten with strong bobby pins, and I smudge the makeup on and pull the long hair across my face. Then I wrap in the blanket, and fasten it with a pin. There is a mirror over the one sink in the change room. I peer at myself. "Molly?" I whisper, wondering if I am indeed in this character. The character just shakes her head, and a raspy sound comes from her throat. All she can do now is sit by the city gate and beg, holding out...holding out...I spy an old metal dish, probably intended for soap. It's perfect.

I leave my shoes and knapsack in the room; I don't want anything to give me away.

For the first time in weeks I don't hesitate outside the door. I take up residence just inside the doorway, and rattle the quarters I've put in the bowl.

A few turn to look at me. Julian is a harlequin, in a wonderful, gaudy peacock costume, his upper face completely hidden but he can't hide his Chesire grin. I give him no sign of recognition, though. I avoid eyes altogether. Can't imagine a medieval-time beggar looking anyone in the eye.

Just as I'm realizing how little I really know about the time period of my character, in walks Ms. Tanaka. I can't help but catch her eye, for a second, before I look away. Her heels click across the floor and I hear her stop on the other side. I steal a look at her, peering from behind the wild wig hair, and find her eyes on me, her expression one of puzzlement. I catch my breath. She doesn't know me!

I feel as if my metal bowl is suddenly filled with gold pieces.

And I feel as if I can't do a thing with any of the wealth.

The class is small today with several people away. A half-dozen others are like me: no one can figure out quite who they are, although, as they begin to speak, we discover their identities.

Julian does an impromptu, jolly dance-slash-acrobatics routine, purposeful tumbling about and comic face-pulling.

He has everyone laughing in moments. I don't laugh; I'm in character. My beggar-child is solemn: life for her is nothing to laugh at.

"What does our beggar do?" Ms. Tanaka's voice cuts through the straggling end of laughter. All eyes turn to me.

A gargling sound comes from my throat. I indicate that I can't speak.

"Okay," says Ms. Tanaka softly. "Our mute beggar from long ago times, what do you do?"

I rise from the floor so slowly, the bones of my left leg shattered by a horse and cart and healed badly by time. I reach for Katherine's broom – she's a Halloween witch – and use it as a crutch. I hobble from one classmate to the next, and proffer my bowl. There is not a flicker of recognition in any of their eyes. They do not see Molly Gumley.

A few throw in a penny or a nickel. "I'll give you a song," says Julian, when I come to him, and he begins to sing 'Greensleeves.' Katherine joins him, with the voice of a crone, and they sing a cappella to the end. I look directly into Julian's eyes. I'd thought if anyone was going to recognize me, it would be Ms. Tanaka or Julian. Does he? The last words of the song pass his lips. He squints. Then recognition is there. He smiles, Chesire grins, and I pour the collection of coins at his feet and hobble back to my place by the door.

The characters do their stuff: the karate guys, their chops; the cabdriver with the unlit cigarette hanging from his mouth sits behind his invisible wheel and gives rides; Katherine takes off the black cape and underneath is the costume of a little girl trick-or-treater. Then the day is over, and everyone is hurrying down the hallway to their lockers. I make my way slowly to the deserted change room. I feel as if I couldn't hurry if I wanted to, I am so slowed by the character.

I sit for a moment on a bench in the murky light, then pull off the wig. I remember being a little girl wearing this wig, entertaining my family. What was the joke I used to tell? "Why are ghosts such bad liars? Because you can see right through them." I used to laugh so hard at that, even when I didn't know what it meant.

The door squeals open and Ms. Tanaka stands there. "It *is* you," she says, and steps into the room. The door slowly closes on the light from the hall. "I was hoping you'd make it, just once this week. Our deal's still on, then." She seems pleased. She picks up the wig. "Amazing. You were so hidden under all this." She puts the wig on herself and looks at me. I look at her: she still looks exactly like Ms. Tanaka, except with long bushy hair.

"You have a wonderful ability, Molly." She pulls off the wig and holds it in her hands.

I don't want to hear this; I can't live up to it.

"You can become a character. Your face, your entire body, metamorphoses. I think even if your beggar character had spoken, I'm not at all certain I would have recognized you."

Her voice drops to a whisper. "Don't give up on the stage, Molly. You belong there."

*That's what I used to think.*

"I don't want to work with your puppets," I say.

She gives me an odd look. "Yes, I see that now. But you do know where you should be." She goes back to the door and stands, with her hand on the handle. "Now that I think of it, you hardly needed a costume today."

*Except that without it, my knees would be shaking and that sick feeling would still be in my stomach.*

Ms. Tanaka asks suddenly: "Do you believe in Santa Claus?"

"I'm fourteen," I say.

She smiles then. "Of course." She moves as if she's about to go, then changes her mind.

"My nephew, Syl," she begins, "I've always taken him to visit Santa Claus. Year after year, these old men-out-of-work actors, I always think when I see them — with the required wrinkles and the spectacles. Some of them even have real bellies. I always imagine that the hiring person for the mall must be absolutely delighted to find an actor with a genuine flowing white beard.

"Then one year, there was this youngish man — 'desperate actor,' I thought, when I first saw him. All he had going for him was a little bit of natural grey in his light brown hair, and he couldn't even keep it from peeking out under his red hat.

Such a horrible false beard. I was so afraid curious Syl would give it a good tug, and I wasn't sure I was up to the questions that would follow." She checks to see if I'm following her story. "There wasn't a wrinkle on his face. Probably had pecs and abs under that red suit. But my nephew didn't notice any of that. And I looked into the man's face and saw why. His eyes. Clear and twinkly and so kind. I listened to his voice as he spoke with Syl, and I heard his words. I saw how his arm encircled Syl, sitting on his knee. Suddenly, I could feel tears in my eyes — made me wonder about myself! But that young man had Santa in him. Unlike all those old fat guys, this man *was* Santa Claus. He had the ability to believe. I think I've believed too, ever since."

She stops then and laughs self-consciously. She swings open the door. "I'll see you Monday. I hope."

"Yeah," I say.

The room is gloomy dark, but only for a moment before the door swings open once again, and a rather flustered-looking Ms. Tanaka appears. Or at least her head and shoulders do. "Molly," she says with hesitation, "I do wish you'd try. Just one more time even. You owe yourself that."

The room seems even darker when the door closes on the teacher the second time.

I put every piece of costume into the plastic bag, and before I leave the school grounds I drop it into one of the dumpsters in the parking lot.

## 19
# A One-Two Thing

om's taken the bucket of cranberry paint she bought for her library and she's painting the bathroom on the main floor.

She won't be upstairs for a while. I find the No Place site again.

*The Get Away From It All,* the caption reads. Uh huh.

I click the email option, and begin my note. I sign it FROM IT ALL.

An hour or so later and Mom's still in the bathroom. I check the email and there's no note from Early. I type *Dear Uncle Early*, write another, and feel as if I'm not connecting at all.

From downstairs, I can hear Mom singing while she paints. Mock opera echoes from the bathroom. She'd be dead embarrassed if she thought anyone was listening; it's worse than her cello even. Still, it cheers her up.

I type one last note: *We're all a part of you, Uncle Early. How far do you think you can run from that?*

O ne: there's no return email Saturday.
  Two: Sunday, there's a note: *Early Hyland checked out yesterday. Left no address.*

Even though it's late afternoon, Mom is sitting at the table behind a newspaper. "Mom," I say, but she doesn't answer. I call to her again. I'm starting to wonder if it's like one of those cartoons where you see fake hands attached to metal 'arms,' attached to clamps, attached to the table, and the person is gone. Gone looking for her brother, the long lost Early.

Okay, not long lost. But it is beginning to feel that way. "Mom?" That's the third time, and still no response. I tap the paper sharply with my fingers and she jumps, yelps, coffee douses both of us. Luckily, it's as cold as last week's.

"How long have you been sitting here?" She looks at me as if trying to remember who I am. "Long enough to read every word twice through," she says, and folds the paper away. "And can't think what a word of it said."

I help her clean up the coffee. I think she's happy to have something to do. She gets on her hands and knees and swipes away at the floor, going farther and farther from the coffee scene. She's reminding me of Early and his attempt at floor washing, and the same thought must be going through her head because all at once she sits back with her bum on her heels and starts to cry.

"Three weeks," she says. I put my arms around her and they feel like sticks. This is new. I've never comforted her like this. Never needed to. Who held her like this when my father died? Early? Grand? Did I give her toddler hugs? My arms turn to rubber, soft, and I hold her.

She wraps her arms around me, tight, and at last gives a pronounced sniff and releases me. "Damned brother of mine," she says, wiping her face on her sleeve. "I've even had to call a detective."

"A detective?"

"I always knew he'd go away without a word."

I suspect that a person in this situation is supposed to try to be calming, and say something like: He'll be okay, he'll send us a postcard. But I have a feeling that if I say that she might sort of blow up. She's an odd shade of red.

"What did the...detective say?" In my mind I see a double-flapped Sherlock Holmes hat, a magnifying glass...no, maybe binoculars, and the Bug beetling down alleyways in a high speed car chase.

"He suggested I wait awhile. Especially after I said yes, my brother's an independent person. He sounded busy, impatient." Another loud sniff, and she's on her feet.

"We'll find him, Mom. We will." *Unless I've chased him farther away.*

She takes a quick look at me when I say this and points a finger at me. "Right," she says. Maybe she wanted to be convinced. She blows her nose, and then heads upstairs. "I'm off. There's work to do. Somebody's numbers to count."

I clean the kitchen. Dishes into the sink, out of the sink, into the cupboard. Wipe the counter. Mom's fussy about the taps and faucet, so I give them a spray and swipe. Tabletop. Finish the floor.

If you plod slowly, but evenly, methodically through housework, it creates a rhythm in you. A one-two sort of thing. Nothing complicated. Just enough to keep thoughts away. Round the corner to the laundry closet. Pull clean clothes out. Refill with clothes from washer. Fill washer with new load. Soap. Turn dial. Water dribbles in and next to it the dryer thrums. Then fold, fold the clean clothes. One-two, one-two. Fills the mind with grey. Not a bad thing really. Maybe I can do *this* for the rest of my life. Maybe this is how it is with Mom and her numbers. I've never understood what Mom does, burying herself in numbers, numbers. But maybe that's what it's all about. I can do that instead of...*Don't go there.* As soon as I stop the one-two pace, the thoughts come leaping from the corners, willy-nilly, spill over each other. *Me, on stage. No.* There's a scuffling noise at the front door. The local paper, probably. But there's no THUMP against the door, the papergirl's trademark. There is a fuzzy knock. Someone is at the door and doesn't really want to come in?

I open the door, and I don't know who is more surprised, me or Uncle Early.

"Trying to make up your mind about whether or not you wanted to knock?" Another surprise, how angry I feel.

He starts to speak but we're both interrupted by Mom, who's come downstairs.

"Early!" Mom's standing at the bottom of the stairs.

My uncle raises his hands. "Will you forgive me, Tessie?"

There's a brief pause. "I usually do, don't I?" she says.

He must be choosing to ignore the new tone in her voice. Or does he really not notice? He says, "You didn't think I'd go away forever, did you?"

*Careful, Uncle Early.*

Mom blinks.

Uncle Early gives me a sudden rib-crushing hug. "You're a powerful letter writer, Mally-girl," he whispers. Then loudly, "Where's the fridge? I've been driving for hours." He heads for the kitchen.

Mom follows. "Where were you?" I can hear.

I hang back for a moment, feeling as if I've been spun in circles, feeling as if I don't like this guy very much.

"Oh, you know." He pulls an apple out of the produce drawer. "Same place as always — no place in particular." He winks at me, then bites into the apple and makes a choking sound. "What the...?" He's almost swallowed the sticker on the apple.

"Small parts are a choking hazard," says Mom dryly. "Wash your food before you eat it."

He stares at her. "You're such a mom."

She looks right back at him. "You're such a..."

The doorbell interrupts.

"Oh, no," whispers Mom. "I forgot. It's Sunday, isn't it?" She doesn't move to get the door.

Early mumbles words with a question mark on the end, and waves his half-chomped apple in the direction of the door.

Then there's a knock.

Early begins to move, but Mom's words stop him. "It's Candace. And Avery. I invited them for the evening." Her voice drifts as Early halts, turns, and then, apple still in hand, flees up the stairs.

Mom looks after him for a second. "Wimp!" she mutters. "He comes back, and then the music starts, and he can't dance!" She opens the door and in the murky outside light stands Candace, looking confused. Behind her, Avery speaks. "Is that...Early's car in the drive?"

Mom's voice is weary. "It is. He's come back." Candace steps into the house, but her mom stays on the porch. Her eyes rest on me a minute, then on Candace, back to Mom. "Come on, Mom," says Candace. "You're freezing the place."

Avery comes in. I notice how she examines the living room, looks up the stairs. But after almost half an hour, Early's plan is obvious: he's going to hide upstairs all night.

Mom warms apple cider, and Candace and I make popcorn with too much butter. The house smells of cinnamon and cloves. Avery builds a fire, and we drag up chairs, move the couch closer.

Avery chooses the seat farthest from the stairs, and after yet another furtive glance in that direction, she rests her feet on the hassock. "It's nice to have more than two bodies in a house," she says, her eyes semi-closed. Beside me, Candace stiffens.

"What's wrong with two bodies?" she asks.

Avery opens her eyes and looks at her daughter. "Especially when one of the bodies decides to move next door."

"The *garage* is not next door," grumbles Candace.

"Might as well be."

Mom clears her throat. "I think the cider is ready."

I offer to help.

"No," she says. "You stay here." *In case a fight breaks out?*

"I'll help." Early's on the stairs. "The cider smells too good," he adds apologetically.

"It is too good," is Mom's quick return. *For you.*

Mom takes her seat, as Early crashes mugs and spoons in the kitchen. We hear a splash of cider on the floor.

"I've never heard him like this," Avery murmurs.

"No," says Mom, but she sounds unsure. "No, not often."

Early enters, sets a tray on the coffee table, sits, and then there's this awful silence. I look at the flames in the fireplace. I don't want to see Early and Avery look at each other. There's something big and painful in the room. Something I know, and my best friend doesn't. It's too much. The feeling of not liking my uncle is washing over me again.

"How about we roast marshmallows over the fire?" Something in his voice now reminds me of the Early I love.

Mom looks suspicious, then she can't stop a half smile. Roasting marshmallows is one of Mom's absolutely favourite things. If Early was somebody else's uncle I'd think it a ploy, but I know my uncle. He does speak with his heart. Just that his heart never seems to be going in the right direction. I swallow the lump in my throat. It's not comfortable, having two feelings about the same person, and the two feelings poking at each other.

"Charades!" says Candace. "Let's play charades."

Now?

"Charades, yes!" says my uncle. He seems so relieved. So am I: we've played charades before; it's something familiar.

"You first," says Mom to Early.

"No, no, the girls can go first," he says.

Mom scowls at him.

"I'll go first," I say. It's old habit speaking. Four pairs of eyes are on me as I move to the clear space between the couch and a chair. My legs feel a bit first-day-at-school shaky. I don't want to perform. I want to recreate a time when things weren't like they are now. I stare out the darkened window for inspiration, but all I see are four hopeful faces.

Only four. Who's missing? *Grand.*

Her birthday tea early last spring. We were all together, the sun was shining. There was green growing everywhere. Someone in your life dies, and you think you miss them in a particular way, and time passes and you find you miss them in another way.

I miss you now, Grand. I miss how life was a Grand Show with you, and without you there's just this winter brown stuff going on.

I pick up Mom's cardigan from the back of the chair, and do up the top button. Early recognizes. "Grand," he says softly.

I stoop, ever so slightly, one eyebrow up, the other pulled down by the mild stroke she'd had. I can't see my own eyes, but I imagine them to be bright, as hers always were, and they *feel* bright. I hear Mom suck in her breath as I look directly at her.

"You've come to my tea," I say, and a slow smile spreads over Mom's face. "Of course, wouldn't miss it, Grand," she'd said that day.

Nobody pointed out to Grand that she was the one who'd done the coming. The tea was at our house, not at the Home. But where Grand was, there was her castle. Or her stage.

And then I remember something, something I hadn't thought about much at the time. Hadn't thought about at all, but now it seems terribly important. Even though it wasn't

Grand's home and she wasn't the host, it was so very typical of her that she took over. But the truth was that she'd acted as the hostess — she had served all of us. And that wasn't typical. This memory is just like the memory of the plaid robe. It's a memory I want to hold on to.

So I follow her steps into the kitchen and I fill the kettle with water. I find teacups, not mugs, and set them on a tray. I put sugar and milk in all of them. Just as she had done, I bark at Mom: "Where's your *white* sugar, Tessa Rose?"

Mom comes into the kitchen then, and her face is crumpled a bit, and a bit shiny, too, in a good way. With a funny little smile on her face, she reaches into the back of the cupboard where she's always kept the covered pot of white sugar, just for her mother. "Here," she says softly. And I can see in that moment that she does mourn her mother. She does miss her. She does have a spot in her heart for her, even though it was never easy.

The sugar is lumped together and I have to scrape at it to put it into the cups. I make the tea and bring it into the living room, and we drink together. Uncle Early takes his cup by the handle, holds it carefully. Takes his time before setting the cup back on the tray.

I look at the faces around me as we finish. "You're amazing, Molly," says Avery. "It's as if she's with us again, just for a moment."

Early shakes his head at me, and there's such warmth in

his eyes. I'm liking him again. The painful feeling is smaller, as if he's taken some of it away.

Mom has that glow she gets when she thinks everyone around her is feeling good.

"I'll get the marshmallows and sticks," says Uncle Early.

For this moment, there's a feeling of "how it should be." The feeling stays as we turn marshmallows over coals — Candace and me and Mom, anyway. Avery's eyes are closing again. Early's humming snags of Simon and Garfunkel tunes. He can do that: make a sort of hole with his hum and crawl right into it, farther and farther away. I can feel it, and see each of Mom's anxious peerings from Avery to Early. The "how it should be" feeling starts to shrink.

Candace burns her marshmallow.

"Too close to the fire," says Uncle Early. "About this far." He illustrates with his fingers. "Keep it that far from the coals, not the flame, and turn it slowly."

I remember this lesson of his from when I was little. "The perfect marshmallow is worth waiting for." That's what he's always said.

Candace concentrates on the marshmallow at the end of her stick. She doesn't look behind her at my uncle as he speaks; she doesn't see her mom's face. Avery is watching Early. Even though her eyes are now more open than they've been all evening, she looks even more tired.

It's not "how things should be"; it's just "how things used

to be." There's no going back. It's different now. There's only going ahead, whatever that means, and it's as if we all have the same thought at the same time: Avery says something about going home; Mom stands and yawns; Early picks up the tray of mugs and bowl and exits. Candace turns around then. "Where's everybody going?"

"Home," says Avery softly.

"My marshmallow," Candace begins to protest.

Avery pulls on her coat. "Looks done to me."

I can't sleep. I'm awake for what feels like hours. Then when I do fall asleep, I dream of laughing faces – Uncle Early, Mom, Avery, Candace – all around me. Each face is a little different, a little changed. I can't say just how. Maybe like a funhouse mirror, but one that works so that the faces are filled out, or narrowed, absolutely right for each. They're laughing and clapping. They're happy. I bow, and I'm happy too. A happy that goes deep, reaches right into me, wraps like ivy around my pelvic bone and grows through my limbs, green vines exploding from my fingers and toes. The vines are like cables, pulling broken pieces back together.

I awake. And I know that it is with this feeling that I want to live my life. Not with that one-two rhythm or with grey blankness.

Just one thing: I don't know how.

# 20
# As Gumley

**C**ome *on,*" says Candace later. "It's Julian's idea." A memory flits through my head, a little ghost with straggly ends. *Remember when you thought it was you Julian liked?* And here he is suggesting I join his and Candace's date because I'm alone and it's Halloween, and he's a nice guy.

"All right, I'll come."

"It's a costume dance, of course," she says.

Hadn't thought of that. *Of course.*

Hmm. "I'll come as me," I say flippantly. Reality: I'll spend an hour in the costume trunk, looking for something.

"I like that," says Candace. "Molly Gumley as Molly Gumley."

"Yeah, what you said." Will I ever be okay with that name?

"We'll pick you up at seven thirty."

Sometimes I go shopping and I know exactly what I'm looking for. I get there, and there's nothing. That's how it is with the costume trunk tonight. Pieces, one after another, and nothing I want.

My words come back to me. *I'll come as me.* I was being silly but now it looks like my only option.

I open my dresser. What's the most me I can be? Top drawer, underwear. I like them slightly baggy, full cut, like an old lady's. Very white, clean, very soft. And no flowers. Took Mom awhile to get that through her head, though finding a stack of unopened packages at the bottom of my closet helped. She got pretty excited, as the topic of money will do for her, but after I pointed out that she could save dollars by never buying flowers, she was quiet. Took the packages and replaced them.

Socks. Okay, here's pattern: red and white, snowflake-like.

Closet. Overalls, baggy. Not too baggy. Just so. Turtleneck. Black or mustard? Dark green? Settle on red. All very dance-able. Amongst two hundred French maids, pop stars, punk rockers with spray-painted hair. Maybe they'll think I'm a scarecrow who lost her stuffing.

"I thought it was a costume dance," says Mom, looking perplexed as I scoot by to answer the door. But she registers shock when she sees Candace, dressed in her mother's clothing, complete with round, hard belly.

"A basketball," says Julian. He taps the hollow rubber, and grins. Candace has a grimness to her, though, and I notice she inches away from him.

"Oh my," says Mom. "Does your mother know you borrowed her clothes?"

"I've been borrowing her clothes for the last two years," replies Candace.

"I would have thought you'd given that up in the past few months, though."

Candace just wraps her arms around the basketball — "protectively" is the word that comes to my mind.

"Well," says Mom, sounding like she wants to convince herself of an idea, "I'm glad it's just a basketball. Not too many night feedings for them, I've heard."

The banner over the doorway says HALLOWEEN DANCE, and underneath, by the door, is, indeed, a fake punk rocker with an electric blue wig and studded plastic jacket.

The rocker turns, and oh my...it's old LUNCH MONITOR. Even Julian sucks in his breath.

"Will you get a load of that?" For once he really does whisper.

"I have this theory," I say, "that people dress up as something they'd like to be."

Candace gives me a sharp look.

"You can be the exception," I reassure her.

"And what about you?" she asks.

"I don't have a choice, do I?"

"But that would mean"– Julian's voice is still low – "that there is hope for LUNCH MONITOR."

The woman is staring at us suspiciously, and he breaks off his words to smile at her, raises his hand. Then he mutters to Candace, "I hope you don't have that whittling knife on you!"

The fake punk is handling our money, and seems to take delight in stamping our hands with a purple-inked fluffy Easter rabbit. "A bit confused," comments Julian as he guides our way through the crowd. He's tall enough to put an arm comfortably on Candace's shoulder, and I don't know which of us is more shocked when she shrugs it off. Even Candace is, judging by the rather desperate look she sends me.

"I'll go find something to drink," Julian mumbles and I nod. When he's gone, I turn to Candace. "Why'd you do that?" I ask.

She doesn't answer me. I notice a couple of guys and a girl looking at her, one curious, another with a mean smirk.

What's eating Candace tonight? Before I can ask, I hear a low voice.

"Hey, I like your costume." I turn and there's Caleb.

Candace is looking away, so she misses his motion toward

her. "Is your friend all right?" he asks softly. I move closer to Candace, who's now examining the floor, and nod.

Then there's just a silence, and finally he says, "Well, I do."

"Do what?"

"Like your costume."

I feel warmth steal over my face.

"Yours, too," I say witlessly. He's dressed as an old western bank robber, ten-gallon hat jammed on his head, 'kerchief over his face, though he's pulled it down to speak to me.

He does a quick-draw, pulls a carrot and a broccoli crown from the holster at his waist.

His face flushes as he does, but he does it anyway.

I laugh. I can smell him: like just-baked bread and the fresh first burst of perspiration on a summer's day. A surprising smell. I can't help but smile.

He takes a breath. "Want to dance?"

I look out to the dance floor, to the three girls in the middle of it.

"Maybe in awhile," I say without thinking.

"Okay," he says, backs into the wall, and hurries away, his face pretty much like the glowing pumpkins in the corner.

*He's not going to ask again, is he?* I hadn't meant anything by that; I'd really *meant* 'maybe in awhile.'

"Wow," says Candace. She sniffs, pats her basketball. "And I thought I was scaring people!"

"Happy Halloween." Julian returns and hands us each a plastic glass of punch. "Did I see Caleb running away from here?"

Candace takes her glass and holds it up to the light as if debating whether or not to have it lab tested. Her face is all wrinkled up when she finally takes a sip. "You guys are always running," she says flatly. "Do you know Molly wanted to chase you that first time we met?"

Julian looks taken aback. "I know she sure can holler after someone. I thought maybe she wanted my autograph." He laughs uneasily. "Or maybe to fingerprint me."

Candace shakes her head impatiently. "You bumped into me, knocked my stuff everywhere."

"*I* knocked your stuff?"

She nods. "You."

"I didn't mean to. I'm sorry." He seems sincerely contrite. For a moment. Then: "Hey! What's with the 'you guys?' You're not doing the Gross Generalization thing, are you?"

Candace crosses her arms

"Are you trying to have a fight here?" Julian asks her. "Haven't you heard? It takes two..."

She glowers at him. Her arms, over her belly, now push the basketball off to one side and it looks ridiculous. Julian tries hard to hide his grin as he adjusts it for her.

Candace pushes his hands away, and he becomes the Lion from *The Wizard of Oz*, trying to be tough, paws folded in the air. "Lemme at 'em! Lemme at 'em!" I start to laugh, but Candace is striding away and, with a shrug at Julian, I follow.

She gets her jacket and my sweater, and I'm aware suddenly of eyes on me: Caleb's, from the far side of the room. I'm sure they follow me all the way to the door.

When we're outside Candace speaks. "Can't even have a decent fight!"

"Did you and your mom…"

"No!" She cuts me off. "No. My mother just went into this long explanation of how sometimes things change. How love can be "elastic" and can stretch to hold more people. Or something dumb like that!" She pulls the basketball from under her shirt and holds it in her arms. She sniffles after a bit, and I put my arm around her waist – I'm not tall enough for her shoulders. *Don't even think of shrugging me off.*

# 21
# Just Off Stage

"**W**ell? What do you think?" Candace's face reminds me of the Itsy Bitsy Spider book I had when I was a preschooler. *Out came the Sun and dried up all the Rain...* I can see the rays shining from her. In her hands she holds a round wooden shape. She passes it to me, and as I take it and feel the warm smoothness of the wood, I realize it's something like a head.

"Nose?" I say, pointing and questioning. "Eyes?" Although at this point they're only shapes, protrusions.

She's nodding furiously. "I started last week. Nan let me bring her home for the weekend. She's for you. When I'm done with her, of course." Candace's voice has hit a new peak.

"Her?" I ask.

"Can't you tell?"

I look at the head. "Nope." I hand it back.

And just like that those rays fade. Right in front of me, Candace shrinks. Her eyes darken. She seems to be squinting, trying to see something in me. "What?" I demand.

"You could give her a chance. She could grow on you. She'd be all yours — not Ms. Tanaka's," she says, and then I realize what she's doing.

"I told Ms. Tanaka I don't want puppets. Any puppet."

Candace just wraps the head in a piece of old soft towel. I almost wish I could take back my words — the disappointment on her face is plain.

Mom comes in from the kitchen, wiping her hands on a cloth. "Would you like to stay for dinner, Candace? Seeing as your mom has her class tonight. I made Hungarian stew with gingersnaps crumbled over it, as you like."

"Yes, please!" says Candace. We follow Mom.

Candace pokes at her stew. "I wonder if my mom's learning anything new at that prenatal class. You'd think going through having a baby once would be enough."

"You think, eh?"

Candace doesn't seem to catch the little laugh in Mom's voice. She just goes on and breaks a piece of garlic bread. "I've been reading about it."

"You have?" asks Mom.

"Candace reads about everything," I remind Mom.

Candace's mouth is quite full and we can hardly understand her closed-mouth mumble as she waves her fork at me. "Stage fright, too."

It's my turn to be surprised.

"Everything," she repeats, nodding. "Do you know Sir Laurence Olivier experienced stage fright?"

*Grand's Saint Laurence.*

"When he was young?" Mom pulls up a chair.

"No." Candace is the voice of authority. "When he was older. After he'd been acting for years."

"What did he do?" asks Mom.

"I haven't read to that part yet," Candace says. "I'm reading about Braxton-Hicks, these early contractions that my mom's getting once in awhile."

Mom smiles. "I remember those. They were so strong when I was pregnant with Molly, that I thought she was going to be early, but no..." She looks as if she could talk about this for a while. I have to interrupt.

"How long was it?"

"Not long," says Candace. "The best thing to do, the book says, is to walk around. Then they go away. Unless of course they're real labour contractions..."

"Candace! Olivier! How long did his stage fright last?"

"Oh that. Seven years."

"Seven *years?*"

She nods.

Seven years. Half my lifetime.

She goes on. "And do you know some actors throw up

every time they go on stage! Maureen Stapleton had hiccups. Every night, every performance, hiccup, hiccup, hiccup, all the way through. At least you didn't do that."

I can hear Uncle Early. *The knocks. Grand couldn't take the knocks of stage.* Is this what he meant?

"None of that matters now anyway," I say. "I've quit. I told you."

"You can't, Molly," says Candace. "It didn't last forever for Olivier. You can't quit just because it happened once."

*Twice.* "I can," I say. I stand, pick up my plate and carry it to the counter. "I've got math homework. You have homework, too." I put my book on the table, find my page, and pretend not to see her mouth open in protest.


The phone rings. My clock glows in the dark: 11:34. Then Mom's at the door, sounding sleepy and mildly annoyed. "It's Candace."

Candace speaks in her I-don't-want-Mom-to-find-me-on-the-phone voice. "I read more," she says. "Olivier had a friend just offstage, but where he could see him."

"For seven years?"

"For seven years."

I think about this a minute.

"Molly?" Candace breaks my silence.

"Mmhmm..."

"I could do that," she says. "I could stand just offstage and send you good thoughts."

I imagine Candace travelling with me, always just offstage, people stepping over her, me packing her into a suitcase, her lugging around a piece of wood so she can carve while she sits there hour after hour, giving me reassuring smiles – or grinning like a fool. Finally somebody'd send her away: too many wood chips, nobody could take it anymore.

"Candace, you can't do that."

"I could," she insists. Then: "Carly Simon took some pills to help her with stage fright."

"Carly Simon?"

"A singer. She's terrified of performing."

*Pills. Sounds easy. Like a vitamin. Vitamin S for Smiling.*

"But the pills scared her more than the performing, so she stopped."

"Stopped?"

"The pills. They did help her to stop feeling scared, but she stopped feeling anything else, too."

*Okay. Actors can't be robots. Scary pills. Won't do that. No, there's just no way.*

"Candace," I say. "Remember? I quit."

The next Thursday, Early volunteers to drive Candace to her class. Avery and Mom are busy, and he says he needs to find out if an apartment has come up. Candace has the head-bundle tucked under her arm, and I don't ask about it. She doesn't say anything either. We climb into Early's Bug. Mom stands close by, her arms folded over her chest. Is she afraid we're all going to disappear now?

"Um...Tess," Early says finally, "you've got to step back. I don't want to run over your toes."

She steps away, but peers at us over her round black sunglasses. She looks like a dragonfly in those. "We'll be right back after Candace's carving class," I remind her. She nods and pushes the glasses back into place. She doesn't go into the house but stands watching as we leave to go downtown.

Usually Uncle Early has a problem with driving teenagers. "I'm not a chauffeur," he says. Today, when Candace and I crawl into the back seat of the Bug, he says nothing, just pulls up the knapsack he always lugs around into the passenger seat beside him, as if to fill the space. After we pull out of the driveway, he says nothing. We begin to yak, yak, yak about school, and what we're doing with the French homework after we get home from carving class, and still Early says nothing. Until Candace mentions prenatal class.

Then Early clears his throat, and we both look at him. I can see part of his face in the rear-view mirror. He's frowning – or at least, his brow is all wrinkled – and he looks as if he has a question he wants to ask. But he doesn't and, after a minute, Candace and I face each other and shrug.

The plan is to drop Candace off at her class, then head east to visit Early's old landlord. When we get there, he has bad news. "I rented your place out just a week ago. If I'd known…"

"See?" I point out. "You could have just phoned."

A harrumph from Early. "Candace needed to go to her class anyway," he says.

We check out another place in the neighbourhood, an old three-storey apartment building, with no luck. Then back to the arts school.

"Guess I'll have to share your couch for a bit, what with all that junk in the spare room," says Early.

"What with all your art collection in the Hole," I remind him quickly.

Another harrumph.

"Do you have a dictionary for those?" I ask. All the variations of *harrumph.*

Early stares at me.

"You might want to watch the road," I say.

He does, and I think he's glad not to be looking at me for his question, "So, how's your mom been with me gone?"

"She phoned a detective to find you." If he wasn't driving I think I might actually hit him.

Early has to straighten out the car because he's almost driven up on the sidewalk. "A detective? No way!" He takes a deep breath. I feel a bit less like hitting him.

"It's the truth," I say.

"What, did she think I was going to disappear completely someday, never to be heard from again?"

"You don't give her any reason to think otherwise. Three weeks this time and next time, who knows!" The words burst out of me.

"What the..." He stares at me, and again I point to the road.

"You two don't know anything about each other," I say. "Obviously."

He just ducks his head, scratches the side of his nose. When we reach the school, he pulls up in front, parks, and sits silently while we wait for Candace. She's late coming out of the door with the bundle again in her arms. She cradles it as she crawls into the car, and she smiles at Uncle Early, but when she looks at me, her smile is apprehensive and she pulls the bundle closer.

All the way home I wonder what words I can say to dispel the witch I was last week, and while I'm thinking, Candace and Uncle Early talk. It goes like this:

Uncle Early. "How was class?"

Candace. "Good. The teacher was teaching us about the grain of wood, but she let me finish my project while she was talking."

Early. "So...you're enjoying it."

Candace (sounding mystified.) "Yes."

Another throat clearing. He starts to say something, then stops.

Is he losing his mind?

"How is your mother these days?" he says, sounding like somebody's grandmother.

Candace looks at me as if to ask, "*What's* the matter with him?"

I shake my head.

She frowns. "Mom is *exhausted*," she says.

"Oh," says Early. He reaches into his knapsack for his pipe and, without lighting it, puts it in his mouth.

"How's school going?" he asks around the pipe stem.

Candace stares in disbelief. Uncle Early is one of those rare adults who *never* asks about school. At least, not like that. He'll ask about something specific, then he remembers the detail for the next conversation.

"You're talking like her," Candace says.

"Like who?" Early looks in the rearview.

"Like my mom," she says. "Saying nothing."

Early pulls his pipe from his mouth. Then puts it back, and is silent until we're home.

Candace carries her bundle into the house, puts it on the chair next to hers at the table. Mom's already eaten, Early says he's not hungry, and it's just the two of us.

"I'm sorry about last week," I say. "About the head." *Doesn't mean I want it, though. I just can't stand to see your face like that.*

Candace gives me a long look, then places the bundle on the table, pushes it past the steaming bowl of minestrone and toward me.

*No, no, no.* But I have to. I unwrap the old soft towel.

It is beautiful. I'll say that for it.

Candace is an artist. I hold evidence of that in my hands, and when I look at her – she's looking at her work – I see it in her face.

What is it to create in a private place, with no need of an audience? What is it to hold your own work like this, finished and complete, and hand it to someone and say, "Here, look what I've made for you."

I'm just a little envious, and wish madly for a moment that I had a desire like hers instead of the one I do have. Or have had. But I've been too silent for too long. Candace is looking at me now with a veritable stew of feeling in her face: bewilderment, hurt. Her back is stiff with pride.

"It is beautiful," I say, so she knows I don't think otherwise.

I can't quite bring myself to touch the face. The eyes are large and round – a bit spooky in their woodenness. The lips are wide and bright. The skin is not painted; the wood grain spreads wider over one cheek and gives her a whimsical appearance, a little off-centre. *I used the word 'her,' didn't I?* I feel as if I've been caught. Or found. I replace the towel quickly.

What am I supposed to do with this gift? With this head of wood? Truth: the thing gives me a chill that knocks my kneecaps off.

To Candace, a 'thanks' won't mean much. "Maybe you're

right," I say. "Maybe she'll grow on me." But she won't; I know it.

Mom and I stand in the doorway to wave off Candace and Avery. Mom wraps her arms around herself to ward off the cold, and watches as they drive off.

"I wonder if Early wants a cup of tea before he goes to bed," she says. "He seems to be hiding up there."

I'm halfway up the stairs. "I'll ask him," I say. Early's going to have to buy a new bumper sticker. One that reads 'I want to be alone.'

I knock and find him sitting among boxes, looking through photos.

"What are you looking at?"

"Come." He pats the sturdy box beside him.

"Christmas pictures." So my 'own nothing, owe nothing,' freedom-craving uncle is discovering a sentimental streak.

It comes back to me now. "Your New Year's resolution was to stop taking pictures of old dead things and photograph people like you used to. Once upon a time," I add.

"Once upon a time," he echoes, and hands me a folder of eight-by-ten black and whites: Candace testing the turkey stuffing, gravy down her chin; Grand resplendent in her red velvet; Mom with a bottle of glue, repairing a decoration fallen from the tree; Avery, rather winsome and thin, gazing out the window. And I'm in each of the photos, somewhere. I'll bet not one of us expected the camera to snap at each of those moments.

"What happened to your New Year's resolution?"

He reaches for the folder. "People scare me," he says. "Old things are so much safer."

*Sorry I asked.*

"Mom wants to know if you'd like a cup of tea."

He looks disoriented, as if the pictures have taken him away.

"Tea?" Still no answer. "You know, black or green leaves, brew in boiled water, pour into a mug..."

"Candace gone home?" he says instead.

"Yes."

He places the folder in a low box, sets it on top of one of Mom's stacks, finds a bit of dried chamomile on the floor, sniffs it, and tucks it into his pocket. "Tea sounds good," he says. His braid is undone, and his grey hair is wiry, standing out from his head as if trying to run. Does he know how old he looks? He meets my eyes and I turn away, but not before I see what's in his. I guess sadness will make someone look older, too.

In my room I find that Candace has put the head on my bedside table, the neck resting in a wide jar. I sleep facing the wall.

I know those wooden eyes are staring behind me as I dress for school and pick up my books.

I pull my sheet and blanket into place, but gather up the quilt and throw it over the head, bury it in crazy squares. Wonder if Candace will notice if I lose it in the bottom of my closet.

When I get home from school, the quilt is gone. Mom chose today to do a Big Cleanup, and my room is miraculously clean, bed remade with fresh sheets, air changed by leaving the windows open all day. The head is in splendour on the dusted bedside table. Mom's even wrapped a scarf around its neck and popped a knit hat over the smooth baldness. I pull the hat down over her features.

Saturday after breakfast, the hat and scarf are gone and Mom has taped a thick paper comic-strip thought cloud over the head. 'Hi Molly!' it says. I find this when I go upstairs to escape Mom's cello moaning.

I pull at the tape, crumple the paper, watch it hit the wall and fall to the floor. I look at the head; it looks at me. It's not going to make a difference – hat, quilt, paper bag. Whatever I put over those eyes, they're still going to bore right through me. No, not through. Right *into* me.

I do my homework at the kitchen table. Mom's squawks and moans are scary, but I'll take that before what's in my room. Why don't I do what I said and bury the thing in the bottom of my closet? Or perhaps drop it out the window?

Because, no matter what I do, those eyes are still going to be there, watching.

I don't return to my room until bedtime. I turn off my light and lie down, but unlike Thursday night, as soon as I close my eyes, my tiredness is gone. I open my eyes to see the head, streetlight shining bald, and her eyes...they look different somehow. Softer, and I'm glad for that. Deeper though, too, as if...as if...I don't want to say it, not even to myself. I swear she blinks. *No!* I take hold of the jar and turn the face away.

## 22

# Anybody Sick?

onday, Julian finds Candace and me at lunch, though usually he shoots baskets with Caleb and their group.

"Candace told me about the head," he says, and he reaches into his knapsack for an object wrapped in brown paper. "Caleb found this in his dad's second-hand book shop yesterday. He thought you could use it."

I open the package to find an absolutely ancient book. I can barely make out the title, it's so worn. *The Art of Puppetry.*

"Why didn't Caleb give it to me himself?"

Julian shrugs. "I think he felt sort of silly."

Inside there are line drawings of how to hold a marionette, plans for a puppet theatre, and a diagram of lip positions for the ventriloquist. I pick up a few pages that have dropped to the floor, push them back in, probably in the wrong place but I really just want the book out of my hands.

Julian looks anxious. "I've never seen a book like that in a regular bookstore. I told him I thought you'd like it." He glances toward Candace and she smiles reassuringly as she takes the book from my hands and flips through pages.

"This is a great book, Julian. There's so much. Look! 'How to Form a Puppet Troupe,'" she reads. "Imagine that, Molly. You could have your own bus, and travel the country."

"Yeah," I say. "Me and the Wooden Heads. Rock Stars. We'll have our own roadies and wristbands!"

"Oh, come on!" Candace holds the book out to me.

"Thanks, Julian," I manage to mumble. I must sound like an ungrateful bum. I focus on the book so that I don't have to see the dimming of the warm light in his eyes. But I am aware of Candace patting his hand awkwardly, and him turning his wrist so that he can catch her fingers in his. I guess they've made up since Halloween.

Outside the window I see a straggly V of Canada geese, moving south in a big flapping hurry.

Something's pulling at me to stay awake. I toss and turn and wonder if Mom will question me if I sleep out in the hall. If I wasn't so reluctant just to touch that thing, I could stick *it* out in the hall, close the door, pull the covers over my head.

"Maybe if you're good, you'll grow up to be a real girl," I say aloud.

No answer.

*Maybe if I tackle this, I'll grow up to be a real actor.* It's more a thought than even a whisper.

I sit and turn on the light. "See? It's just me in this room." Silence.

I turn off the light, slide under the quilt.



Posters have gone up for *The Sound of Music*. This is the first high school or community production that I haven't gone to see since I was a little Grade 1 kid. Mom offered to buy tickets, and go with Candace and Avery as always, and she looked disappointed when I said no, but she didn't push it.

The morning of opening night, I find Ms. Tanaka, with her coffee mug in hand, looking through some papers on her table. She doesn't see me at first, and doesn't hear me either, even though my heart's beating so loudly I'm sure it's sounding across the room.

Finally, "Oh, Molly," she says, and she pulls off her glasses. "Take a seat." She motions to the torn leatherette stuffed couch nearby, and I sit. Except I can't, so I get back up again.

"What is it?" she asks softly.

"Is anybody sick?" I ask, then realize how stupid that sounds. "I mean, in the cast. *The Sound of Music.* Has anyone dropped out? Do you need someone to fill in?"

She puts her glasses back on. "Why do you ask?"

"I was thinking. If you need someone to fill in, I could. I need to know...if I can do it again." Now I can sit. I need to, because if I don't my knees are going to quit on me.

"I see," she says, and sits staring at me. "You want to try again."

"I need to."

She thinks for a moment. "We do have an extra nun costume. You could be one of the Sisters. I'm sure you know the words to the songs. And you won't have to speak."

She looks at me, hard, and there's that questioning look that I saw in her face the first day of school. "Maybe we can give you a line, though." She squints. "Yes, let's give you a line. Come back at lunch. I'll find something for you."

It all sounds so easy. A costume; one line.

"Thank you," I tell her and hurry away before I change my mind.

"Molly," she calls after me, "I'm glad to see you trying again."


My line: *"How do we solve a problem like Maria?"* I go over the words in my head, again and again.

At home after school I take that head – pick it up by holding the jar – and stuff it in the closet. I try to focus on homework at my desk, but after just a few minutes, I open the closet door again, pull it out, and carry it downstairs and set it out by the back door. "It's not that cold," I mutter to it as the screen door snaps back into place.

*How do we solve a problem like Maria?* goes through my head as I fill my plate with tortellini.

"More homework tonight?" Mom says to make conversation.

Should I tell her? How will I explain when I have to leave for school in half an hour?

"I talked with Ms. Tanaka today." I try to keep my voice casual. "I asked her if there was something I could do tonight...in the play."

There's a sudden shine in Mom's eyes that I'm positive wasn't there a split second ago.

"She said she has an extra nun costume, and she even came up with a line for me."

I can tell she's trying not to seem excited. "I'm glad to see you're trying again, Molly."

"That's what Ms. Tanaka said, too."

"Shall I come to the show?" she asks.

"I think I should do this on my own."

"All right." She doesn't argue. "I'd like to drive you there, though," she says.

When she drops me off at the front driveway, I have a moment of feeling alone. Other cast and crew are dropped off and they hurry toward the door, but in me there's that sense of being completely on my own. I hadn't told Candace my plans. I just want to see if this is something I can do.

Above the sounds of hurrying kids, I can hear the wind in the maple, still with its brittle leaves and wintry branches. It's a cold sound.

I'd forgotten about Julian. Having him there was like having ten of Mom and Candace. "I heard!" he said. "Ms. Tanaka said you'd be here. And I have your costume!" He hands me the black habit and wimple, gives me a one-armed hug and then, to my relief, rushes off to help someone else.

The problem with being one of the chorus is that there's really nowhere private to change. I can see the other nuns in a back corner, giggling and helping each other pin their hair out of sight. With full makeup, they look very unlike nuns. "Girls," says Ms. Tanaka, as she hurries by, "you're not the countess, remember!" And there's some hurried lipstick wiping.

She doesn't notice me in my own corner downstage. I slip the robe over my head and pull my hair back into a tight ponytail. I can hear the band warming up in the pit. I've already applied makeup – foundation, a neutral lipcolour, liner and mascara – at home. I pull the wimple into place.

A clarinet's notes pull out of the straggle of musical melee, and carry the melody of *the hills are alive with the sound of music...* I suddenly wonder what I am doing. I sit with my back to the black wall at the foot of the curtains. I feel small there, but I feel comfortable too, and as if I could be quite happy just staying there, not pushing myself out in front. *Why am I doing this again?* Because I need to know. I need to know this about myself: Can I be on stage?

Then the audience begins to file in, and Ms. Tanaka shoos us all to the drama rooms in back.

There's a table with fruit and water on it, chairs to sit and relax — as if. And a computer screen shows, at this point, an empty stage. A lighting guy runs across it to fix something. Audience heads bob by. Some wise guy makes a face at the camera and sticks out his tongue.

The clock on the wall, right next to the TV, reads ten minutes to the hour.

Beside me, Maria von Trapp hums. She's the Grade 11 Jar Jar Binks ponytail girl. She seems to be one of those sweatpants types, and I've wondered if she ever stood out before this pro-duction. I've heard people in the halls talking about her voice, so I know I'm not the only one surprised. Now she smiles at me in a very governess sort of way. "Glad you're here with us tonight!" she says in a warm voice. I wonder if this is something she's always wanted. Or if being on stage is new, unexpected, a turning point in her life. She's not new to singing, I know that.

"Thanks," I say.

"Can't believe it's opening night already," she goes on,

fiddling with the apron around her waist. "Everyone's coming to my house after — wanna come?"

"That sounds good," I say, trying not to sound hesitant. I don't want to think about "after."

Even through the closed doors, the sudden crash of the music is loud with the opening notes.

"That's my cue," says the girl, giving a final tug on the apron, and she hurries out.

"Ours is next," calls out one of the nuns, the Mother Superior. "Over here, Molly!" she calls out to me. They've gathered by the door. "Just stick by me!" Mother Superior smiles.

There's an energy in the air that I suspect has everything to do with it being opening night. The nun to my left takes my hand and squeezes. I don't know who knows my story and who doesn't. But the hand clasp and the squeeze make me feel like pulling away, running away. I force myself to stand exactly where I am, and after a half minute, she releases me.

Superior is by the open door. "Almost..." she says, looking at her watch. I can feel dampness between my shoulder blades, sweat. My stomach is heavy.

I try to think back to being in the Christmas town pageant when I was five. It was a show in the local shopping mall. How I'd breezed onto stage for my part. Then flash forward to being eight, in the drama camp. Then Dorothy and "Somewhere Over the Rainbow." Grand keeps trying to enter my thoughts but I push her away. I push away the *out there* thought, too.

Then the nuns are all sweeping out the door. I'm moving too and we're heading for the backstage door. The heaviness in my stomach is growing and the sounds around me are muffled as if I'm climbing out of a quilt. We're in the darkness of backstage, then we're in the wings, and I catch sight of Maria with her guitar case, running to the abbey; the lights are suddenly a cold blue, and it's time for us to go out. Blue is our cue. And the heaviness in me is rising, and all at once the front of my habit is warm and there is a pungent odor. Me. Throwing up.

"We'll be okay without you," says the nun who moments ago held my hand.

I almost laugh at that, except tears are coming out of my eyes, as I back up farther and farther, and gather up my habit, pull off the wimple. Then I'm out in the hallway, and sitting on the floor, with all that black fabric balled in my arms.

*How do we solve a problem like Maria? How do we...* How do I do this? I think.

"Here," says a voice, and I look up to see Caleb, holding out a bottle of water. I can't look him in the eye as I reach for it, take a long drink, and then pour some over my forehead. I'm glad when he doesn't say anything. But somebody needs to.

"I don't think I can do this," I mutter finally.

"Maybe not now," he says.

"Maybe not ever," I say.

"Maybe you just need to find a different way to do it." He snaps the lid back on the bottle, and avoids my eyes.

"When I used to go onstage, I could always feel Grand – my grandmother – with me," I whisper.

"And now?" he asks.

"She's gone." I stand, feeling a bit wobbly. "Thanks for the water."

"You're welcome. And I'm sorry about your grandmother."

"I'm sorry about the dance. I was pretty thoughtless."

He nods and shrugs.

"How long have you and Julian been friends?"

Now he laughs. "Since the first day of kindergarten."

"Sort of like me and Candace."

"How are you going to get home?" he asks.

"I'll be fine," I say.

"I'll walk you. But first, I'll let one of the other ushers know." And off he goes.

I don't know how he manages to find my sweater, but he does, along with a bag for the costume. We don't say much on the way home, and it's not until afterwards, safely inside the front door, that I realize he took the bag with him. In the olden days, he would win the status of *gentleman* for that. He would deserve it, too. His words come back to me. *What would be a different way?* I wonder. What would take away the feeling of being so alone? It scares me that, even after yet another try, I still can't seem to back away; some other part of me is still looking for possibilities, even though my mind says, "Don't bother. You're done."

Mom takes one look at my face and plugs in the kettle. Then she gives me a long hug. But neither tea nor hug takes away the hollow feeling inside me.

When I go upstairs to bed, there's an emptiness to the room, too. Takes me a bit to realize it's the head, the missing head, and the cleared top of the bedside table. I think about Candace's carved work, out in the cold November backyard. Maybe part of me is out there, too.

I can hear Mom padding around her room, climbing into bed. She must have left her door open.

I climb back out of bed and pull my door open, too. The glow of her bedside light flows into the hallway and I can see it from my bed.


The damp air isn't good for the wood," says Mom, pouring her coffee the next morning.

The head is in the middle of the table, surrounded by a plate of toast, butter, jam and a jug of milk.

I sit opposite the thing and look at it. Yesterday, I'd woken up with a plan: see if I can be on stage again.

Today I feel as if I need another plan. Even if it's just to deal with this gift from Candace.

Options: Pack it away in a bag and throw it out. Or hide it somewhere I'm unlikely to trip over it. (Like buried in a deep hole in the backyard!) Arrange some flowers in its jar for company.

These options require touching it. How silly is that: not wanting to touch an *object*. A *thing*.

*What am I waiting for?*

Very slowly I reach. The wood is smooth under my fingertips.

*I've been afraid to touch her, haven't I?* I run my hand, then both hands, over the wood, feel the grain of it, the bump of nose. And wonder why I haven't before this.

It takes me a long time to find that book from Caleb. When I do, it's under the pile of clean-but-not-folded clothes to the right of my dresser.

It's Saturday and I know that Candace will be in her "studio" as she calls it. And rightfully so.

"What do you think?" I ask her. "Do you think you can turn it into a dummy? For a ventriloquist?"

"Who's the ventriloquist?" She puts a pair of scissors away.

"Me. I mean, I will be. That is, I'm going to try."

"That's different from a puppet, huh?" But she doesn't wait for an answer. "How'd you come up with that?"

"Something Caleb said."

"Caleb, eh?" she says in a teasing tone, and takes the head from me.

I reach into my pocket for the book. "There're a couple of chapters in here about it."

Candace trades me the head for the book. I sit on her bed, with the head in my lap, and realize that I'm still a bit shaky. It seems like a long time that she looks at the plans in the old yellowed pages. She takes the head to her work table and takes some measurements, then roots around in her containers for bits and pieces of who-knows-what.

"We'll need to sew arms and legs," she says suddenly.

"Maybe your mom will help," I say. Candace frowns at that but continues to read. "Plywood," she mutters, and she leaves her table to clatter down the garage stairs. Up she comes with a few odd bits of wood. But not before I finally notice what she was working on before I arrived.

On the wall opposite the work table is what must be a refrigerator box, opened, painted white, and nailed to the wall. In all that blankness, Candace has begun to paste letters from newspaper headlines. FATHER *dad* PAPA *le pere*. And the question: *What Is A Father?* And other words: *Where? When? Why? What? How?*

Just what does '*how* is a father' mean? My friend suddenly has a whole lot of questions that she's claimed she doesn't have.

And there's the cigar end and the balloon bit, looking like Eeyore's birthday present.

She's busy marking the plywood in some way, but I ask "What's it all going to be about?"

"It's just the beginning," she says. "I'm not sure where it'll go. All I know is that we're all missing dads."

The reminder of my own father catches me by the side of the throat. Then I realize she's used the word 'all' and know that she's including the baby with the two of us. And the next thought: Candace's brother or sister will be my cousin; the thought makes me want to tell what I know.

I stand at her side, watching her draw a pattern.

"Go home," she says. "I can't work with someone hanging over my shoulder. Come back tomorrow."

# 23
# Sneckle

*I*'ve been up all night," Candace announces from the top of the stairs. She runs down to meet me and back up two steps at a time. "Look!" she cries, and picks up two objects from her worktable. Wooden hands.

"They're beautiful." I cradle them in my hand, so smooth and perfect. I can feel the warmth of the wood.

"Did these take all night?"

"Not quite," she says.

Then she holds up the head and I'm startled. The chin has been cut — of course! I should have known. The chin would have to be cut to make it so that she can talk.

Candace pats my arm. "I didn't hurt her. I promise!"

I feel a bit foolish.

"I wanted you to be here for this," she says. She uncovers an object on her worktable, and I see that it's something like a wooden box.

"My mom's finishing sewing the arms and legs. Why don't you go get them from her?"

"All right."

"Then we put the head on and there she is!"

Sounds so simple.

I find Avery working at her desk. She doesn't take her eyes off the computer screen.

"Candace says you've sewn the arms and legs of the dummy."

Avery nods slowly and completes the sentence she's typing. "They're on that shelf there." She motions to the wall.

On the third shelf, I see the pieces. She's stuffed them, too, and there's a spool of thread and needle nearby. On the shelf above I see a bright red little dress and a stretchy pink sleeper with a ruffle around the neck. There's no mistaking that they're clothes intended for a girl, and they look as if they just came from Avery's machine. I pick up the sleeper and turn around to find Avery looking at me. She seems a bit short of breath.

"Those are for my book, 'Sewing For Children.'"

"Oh," I say. Why don't I believe her?

"Here." She comes over, takes the dress from the shelf and hands it to me. "Could you use this? For your dummy?"

"I suppose so."

"It'll save you time." She doesn't move back to her seat but stands awkwardly. I'm getting the idea that the dress is an exchange for something; just what, I'm not sure.

*What do you want, Avery?*

"Candace and you…talk, don't you?" It finally comes out.

"Of course," I say. I'll play dumb.

"No," says Avery, struggling with words. "I mean, talk about *us*…her and me, and the baby."

"Not…really."

She seems so disappointed. Even her belly seems to deflate.

"I tried to talk to her," she begins.

"She says you don't say anything important. Anything that makes sense. And you don't listen." *So maybe we talk a bit…*

She picks up the thread, breaks off a piece for the needle, and says, "I tried, but she didn't seem to want to hear me. Maybe both of us don't want to hear what the other has to say. I know this will be a big change. I wish she'd tell me what she wants."

*How about a baby that turns into a pig and runs away?*

She begins to sew across the top of one of the arms, her whipstitch perfectly even without a thought. "I didn't plan on having a baby when I was forty-four. When I first realized I was pregnant, I was in shock. I didn't know how to tell Candace. I couldn't think what to do. All my careful plans. I'd been thinking about retirement planning." She knots the thread and automatically picks up the second arm. "As the weeks have gone by, the baby has come to seem like a...gift." This time the sound she makes is one of being close to tears. "A gift no one wants to share with me." Her voice is a whisper. "I'd like to come out from behind this big front and show everyone how I'm not sorry at all. How, in spite of being tired and full of questions and no answers, this..." she holds her belly protectively..."this is good."

If it's so good, I wonder, why does it all have to be so secret?

So?" asks Candace. "Was she in the bathroom or the fridge?"

"At her desk. She even sewed up the ends for me."

Candace raises her brows, but I say nothing more.

My mind plays over Avery's words as I begin to attach the legs to the form on Candace's table. Candace is busy attaching the carved hands to the arm pieces.

The body is complete. She picks up the dress. "Cute," she says, but her tone isn't warm. She pulls it over the body, and I feel a tug of guilt. I don't like this — feeling so in-between Candace and her mom. Add Uncle Early, and it's a triangle. After all, he has a big role in this, and neither Avery nor Candace know that I know what that role is.

Candace picks up the head, fits the dowel into the opening. The head drops into place with a soft and final thud.

"That's it then." She seats the dummy on the edge of the work table and steps back, stands still, appreciating her work.

I think of the jelly-bean-red wig in the costume trunk at home: it'll be perfect.

She's more than a puppet, I tell myself, more than a carving. She sits with a hand to one side, the other in her lap, her head up, ears listening. Her bravery takes me by surprise. What was it I'd said? 'Maybe if you're good, you'll grow up to be a real girl.'

But there's such stiffness to her. What did I expect? She's made of WOOD! Why did I think that with a body, she'd have the aliveness she had the night before?

"Something's wrong," says Candace.

"No, no, nothing." I try to smile.

"You thought there'd be magic."

I laugh. Uneasily. Am I so transparent?

"That's up to you," Candace's voice is soft. She hands the figure to me and I hold her in my arms, a plywood corner poking into my ribs, an elbow lumpy. *Her.*

"What's her name?" asks Candace.

"Mortimer." *He was the one who made me laugh the most,* Grand had said of Mortimer Snerd, the funny-faced dummy she'd grown up with.

"You can't name her Mortimer!"

"No. But I could call her...Millicent."

Candace thinks about it for a minute. "The Molly and Milli Show!" she says.

I hadn't thought of that.

"And her surname?" Candace asks.

"How about...Sneckle. Millicent Sneckle." If I have to live with Gumley, she can settle in with Sneckle.

"Sneckle and Gumley. They belong together."

*Make that 'Gumley and Sneckle.'*

Candace ties a length of string around the book to keep the old pages together, and tucks it into my pocket. "You'll need this. Take her home. Get to know her." She motions to the collage. "I have my work to do."

## 24

# Grand Illusion

efore school Candace insists I see the collage. She's been busy. There are pictures now along with the letters, the cigar and the scrap of balloon. It's hard not to notice the pile of parenting magazines underneath. The pages have been ripped out, cut into, and the covers are gone. "People don't keep those things, you know. I found them at the thrift shop, ten cents apiece."

The shiny pictures are of women and children: babies, toddlers, teenagers; young moms, old moms. Every grouping has one thing in common. The father is missing. Candace's exacto knife has removed every strand of hair, every hand on a shoulder. Their absenteeism is outlined with perfection, and the effect makes me feel a sick sadness.

"Where are they all?"

Candace points to a shoebox.

"What are you going to do with them?"

"I don't know," she says, but I think she's faking her carefree tone.

"Let's get outta here." I lead the way.

The chapter on ventriloquism looks too short, and opens with underlined instruction: It is imperative to the art that is ventriloquism that the reader not divulge the following to even those near and dear. The Art is a secret one, and to share it is to betray all fellow artists, and to severely jeopardize the Grand Illusion.

The Grand Illusion. The writer makes it sound almost sacred. Everything is always so serious in old books. I begin to turn the page, but feel someone looking at me. I look up toward the door, but realize it's Millicent's eyes I feel. Big, brown, and staring. I feel humbled and I'm not sure I like the feeling.

But I raise my right hand. "I solemnly swear. Not to divulge the Art."

Do I also feel some stir of recognition? *Oh, let this be my path. Let this be the different way...*

Turn the page and THUNK.

The next page is covered in ancient line drawings and words printed in such small type, I can hardly read them: it's like trying to discover whether a wood bug is a boy or a girl.

ALVEOLAR RIDGE. Isn't that a World War I battle site?

THE VELUM. Whatever that is.

UVULA. Sounds private.

THE LARYNX. That's a bit familiar...

But all in all, BORING.

I turn the page quickly. PROPER BREATHING, is one subtitle. Mr. Roman used to talk about that all the time. "Use your diaphragm to pull the air in, push it out. THE DIAPHRAGM!" he'd shout. And we'd giggle.

Flip through the next few pages. Where's all the good stuff? The stuff about throwing your voice and speaking without moving your lips? Where's all that?

Here's what it does say: *Spend at least four weeks, a quarter of an hour each day working on these preliminary exercises.*

Preliminary, huh? There's only four weeks to the variety show.

*Four weeks.*

The faded black letters blur on the cream-coloured page. The old paper bubbles, turns to pulp as I dab at it. This book can't take tears.

I throw it aside on the bed and glare at the dummy. Candace's creation is all wood now. Her eyes appear flat, her arms and legs hang uselessly. I notice suddenly that the dress fits oddly around her shoulders. The corner of the wooden frame is almost poking through. There'll be holes in the fabric soon.

Beyond my room, the furnace decides the house is warm enough, and shuts off with a clunk.

Mom's out. Early, too. The hush is dead.

I could reach out and turn on the clock radio.

Then clearly, as if she's in the room herself, I can hear Candace say, "You've never had to work hard for anything, Molly. Whatever you want to do, it's easy for you." Her voice hadn't been unkind. She'd just said it straight out. As only a good friend can. I close my eyes to stop the tears, though a few more escape. It had been so easy that I'd never even recognized it for what it was. So it was more a thoughtless thing than an easy one. As soon as I started thinking about it – about what I wanted to do, about being on stage, about *not* being on stage, and all about Grand, and where that left me – BOOM. It blew up in my face and left pieces everywhere. I suppose I could have just left them and walked away – if I could. Instead, I've been scrambling around with the pieces.

I reach for the book. The page has fallen out. I hold it in place and look at it again. So it's not Boring. It's just Not Easy. But it seems to be part of it all – the picking up the pieces – so I'll just have to hunker down and get to it as Mom would say. "The Knocks," Uncle Early had said. This is The Knocks.

First a trip to the bathroom to blow my nose and wash my face. The water is cold and tingles. And the tears did feel good, as if they might be able to mix with a little clay, make a little mortar, meld a few pieces back together.

Fifteen minutes a day, *says the book. Don't strain your voice.*
So I do fifteen minutes. In the morning. During lunch break. After school. And before bed. Four weeks of work in one. I can tell you where the alveolar ridge is, and there are no soldiers climbing over it.

By the beginning of the second week Mom stops looking startled every time I walk into the room saying, "shay-shoo-shay-shoo-shay-shoo" or "oh-ah-oh-ah."

I exhale as I bow and say, "Thanks."

Mom says, "You're welcome."

"I'm not really thanking you," I say. "Just getting rid of stale air."

"You're welcome all the same."

Week Two: tongue exercises. Clicking, sticking it out, stretching. This, I keep to myself. And FINDING THE RESONANT VOICE. Hum an MMMMMM sound. This I do: walking to school; to home; in the hallway, though I don't mean to. It's just becoming habit.

Next day: NNNNNN.

The following day: NGNGNGNGNG.

"Good MMMorNNNiNGNGNG, Mr. Pritchard," I say on Friday. Perfect word that: MORNING.

And Mr. P, always happy to go along, doesn't hesitate. "Good MMMorNNNiNGNGNG, MMMolly!" he says.

"This is something new, then." Exactly what he said to Bryn when he coloured his hair blue, and to Dulcie the time she came into class with headphones and he put them over his own ears and listened for a few minutes.

I've done it – VOICE PRODUCTION – and ready for the next chapter.


Come see this," says Candace at her house later. She's taken all the father cut-outs, glued them to cardboard, cut notches into them, and stood them all over the room.

"They're everywhere," I say. I didn't think this is what she wanted me to say.

"They are, aren't they? And not one where he's supposed to be!"

I touch one and the cut-out falls over. "We don't really know anything about them, do we?"

She doesn't say anything to that. I see a few new items on the white cardboard: a pair of sports socks; a child's handmade Father's Day card, water-stained; an old television remote control. But there is something missing.

"There's this," says Candace. She picks up a wide and ugly necktie and staples it on. She stands back, looks it over, looks at me, chews on her fingertips. "Oh, and this." She holds up a large wooden thread spool, split in half down the middle. "My mom gave it to me and said that Grandpa gave it to her when she was a kid and they played all sorts of games with it." She tosses it back to the floor.

I look at the collage, and try to think of what I have to say about it. "It's just that usually your work makes me see something new."

She stares at the cardboard. "I know," she says shortly.

"This doesn't."

"I know."

## 25
# Difficult Letters

There's something different about Early's Bug in the drive: aha! a new sticker. *If it comes back it's yours!* Wow – that's *old*, Uncle Early. Is that a new dent in the right fender? He'll be grumpy, for who knows how long. Yep, I can hear his voice as I approach the front door. Looks like I'll be able to scoot upstairs with no one noticing, just as I was hoping. He and Mom arguing. Again.

I sneak to my room, sit on the bed, crack open the book. I've been trying to keep up with the mending, but still every time I open it, there's another page coming out. It has to hold together until I have a handle on all this stuff.

There. On the fifteenth page of the chapter. WORKING WITH YOUR VENTRILOQUIAL FIGURE. 'Lifelike Movements,' is one subheading, and 'Voice Contrast' is another. I take Millicent off the bedside table and sit her on my knee.

"You need a little weight there, Ms. Bony Butt," I say.

"Well…" she drawls. Her voice is high, but not falsetto.

"Do you always speak so slowly?" I say.

"Somebody's gotta put some thought into SOME-THING around here!" is her retort.

I'm surprised how full her voice sounds: my practice is paying off.

"Are you saying I don't put much thought into what I say?"

"Well, you're calling me BONY BUTT, yet as I see things, I'm pretty much one of your best friends."

"You might have a point."

"And," Millicent goes on, "you're moving your lips, girl!"

"We'll have to fix that."

"You first," she says.

I turn my attention back to the book, and try to ignore the voices from downstairs. Mom says the word SELFISH clearly. Then something about SCARED. She'll have Uncle Early running from the house again, if she keeps that up.

I read from the crackly old page: *The ventriloquist is, firstly, an actor.*

"Thanks," I say softly. "I'll keep that in mind."

*An actor who must play two roles at once. Practise in front of a mirror. Watch for lifelike, natural movement.*

The book was written before video cameras existed. Actually, *this* book was written before *movie* cameras were invented. But that lends it a sense of the magical. All that stuff about secrets. Makes me feel sacred. Lucky. Grateful.

It is reassuring, that first I must be an actor. I'm still on familiar ground. Like travelling for a long time, then waking up in my own bed.

Voice control and acting. But what about voice throwing, and yes, moving your lips?

Page twenty. There they are: THE DIFFICULT LETTERS. P B V F M W. The letters whose sounds cannot be produced without movement of the lips. Then the thought comes: *three weeks to go.* I may be comfortably back in my own bed, but underneath it there's a thorny monster with bad teeth and his name is Despair. I can feel him getting closer.

"Aw! We don't need those letters anyway! What are you freaking out about?" Millicent peers past my shoulder to the page.

I laugh. "You are pretty good at monster chasing."

"That's what I do best!" She straightens proudly and her head rises ever so slightly from her neck.

"Look!" With my free hand I point out the next line to her. "Here it says to avoid these letters whenever possible. Substitute other words."

The next six pages detail how to produce each sound. PRACTISE PRACTISE PRACTISE is written across the page.

"Can't even say *that!*" grumbles Millicent.

"Hey! You're not allowed to be grumpy!"

"Oh yeah?"

The sentences in the book that are intended for practice are ridiculous. 'Peter Piper' and so on.

Think up a sentence with words that begin with 'P,'" I ask Candace on the way to school next morning.

"Haven't I done enough already?" But before I tell her to forget it, she comes up with: "Polly Poppins popped the pus from her purple pimple."

"That's disgusting!" I shout. "But good!" I give it a try. Sounds a little like pus in ventriloquial tongue.

"How about 'B'?" I ask. I try not to think 'three weeks' but that despair monster is whispering the words over and over.

She barely pauses. "Beg to borrow the Early-bird's beautiful Bug!"

"Not until I'm sixteen. And even then. He'll never let anyone else drive his precious Bug." I stagger over that sentence, the Bs sounding mushy and very much like something else.

"What next?" Candace asks with a wide grin.

"V."

But we're at school now. "I'll think about it and come up with something," she says.

'Ventriloquism is very vexing,' is all I can come up with myself by the end of Humanities class. I look up to see Ms. Frizzelle staring at me, suspicious. That'll be another plus to being able to speak without moving my lips: I can talk to myself any old time without people bugging me. I smile at Ms. Frizzelle and she turns away.

'Frightened Frizzelle fears the follies of frolicking buffoons.' Not bad.

"I've got one for M," Candace says at lunch. "Molly and Millicent make a most marvelous match."

"You think?" I stop tugging at the plastic wrap that covers my sandwich. "Thanks," I say softly. I can hardly hear myself. I clear my throat, raise my voice. "For everything."

"You'd do the same for me," she says, and pops a hot pickled pepper in her mouth. She talks as she chews. "You did do the same for me, finding my woodcarving class."

"That was different." It's easier, doing things for others when you think you're sitting on top of the world. I know that now.

Julian comes by as quietly as if he has stocking feet and, without looking at either of us, he deposits a tiny packet on the table, mysteriously wrapped in brown paper, tied with a green ribbon. "Sspppt!" he says, as if it's a password in some little-kid movie. He glides away, leaves Candace with a half grin on her face. "He's a bit crazy, I think," she says softly. "I've tried very hard not to like him..." Her words drift off as she picks up the packet, and she looks at it with a slight shake to her head.

"Might be something you need," I say.

"Might be." She tucks it into her pocket. "Where were we?" she asks.

"W."

"You have woefully wee weeks to work." She comes up with it so quickly, I have to laugh.

"And it makes me want to weep," I say. But I don't. I have Candace beside me, and Millicent. They give me strength, make me feel that maybe if I open my arms the world will creep in, snuggle up, even stay awhile.


What do you think these are?"

"I dunno."

"They were in that package Julian gave to me." She shows me the slip of paper that accompanied the packet. *'For Your Collage.'*

She moves the objects on her palm. I pick up a sickle-shaped one and turn it around. It looks like...ivory cuttings, is all I can think. Then it comes to me.

"Yuck! They're TOEnails!" I drop it to the floor, and Candace's follow.

I reach for the wrapping. Julian must have something to say about this.

He does. Scribbled inside the paper, he's written *'I SWEAR I washed these. Walked around my house trying to find some PECULIARLY fatherish thing for your collage. Seems I've been tripping over these since I was a little guy. Glue 'em on.'*

Candace hunches over the scattering on the floor. "This is what it's like to have a father in the house, huh?" Her voice is hushed, wondering.

"For Julian, anyway." I look at the clippings, too. "I'm sure not every dad has...the toenails of an elephant, and leaves a trail after him." Candace is giggling even before I finish my sentence, then I'm giggling.

She reaches for her bottle of glue.

"A trail, huh?" she says, and sticks them in a line that wanders across the bottom of the cardboard.

W here do you think you're going, Ms. Gumley?" The voice is stern.

"Home," I say, my mind suddenly scrambling. Is it Friday? It's become a pattern now, hasn't it? Skip drama class, be home early. Attend one class per week. Friday. But, "Today's Wednesday," I say. Foolishly, I'll admit.

Ms. Tanaka's eyes narrow. She closes them as if she has to do that regrouping, count-to-ten thing that stressed adults do: the deeeeeep breath, release negative whatevers.

"I didn't see you last week," she speaks finally. "And we're halfway through this week."

Uh oh.

"We had a deal." She sounds tired.

"I was really busy last week." Talk fast, Molly. "Working on my act for the variety show."

There's not so much as a comma of body language from her. I'm a beetle flailing on the end of a pin here, but I'm not ready to talk about Millicent quite yet, so I'll have to go for the stupid-me tack. "I forgot it was Friday."

"You know I tell my students not to limit themselves." There's a Big Warning in her voice. "Come any day," she says. "Come every day even. But come today and we'll...act as if it's last Friday."

She doesn't have to say this is my last chance.

I move to put my coat and books back in my locker.

"Just bring them with you. It's late." She starts down the hall, obviously expecting me to follow.

I do, and have a sudden vision of Millicent on my arm, her head forward, neck stretched out, her voice high. I can almost hear her singing...what? I know. That old Beatles song about "she loves you, yeah, yeah, yeah." But Millicent's words are filled with sarcasm, coming from her wide open mouth. And the final word "glad" is sung all warbly over a grand finale ending. I giggle.

"What?" Ms. Tanaka turns around.

"Nothing," I say.

## 26

# Crash

"What's with all this?" Uncle Early asks. "Polly Poppins..." His voice drifts off as he reads the sentences I'm writing on heavy paper.

"It's the latest in teen room décor," I answer. *You should see Candace's.*

"You're following something with your nose to the ground." He's not used to me shutting him out. I hand him the masking tape. He can make the pesky little rolls for me. I begin to hang the papers.

He takes in my room: Millicent at her post by my bed; the one and only piece I've resuscitated from Grand's collection — the pic of Edgar Bergen with his dummies, Charlie McCarthy and Mortimer Snerd.

"You haven't quit, have you?" Uncle Early says.

I involuntarily shiver as I hear him say that word. I can instantly recall the challenge in his voice when he first said it.

This time, though, his tone is different: grudging admiration.

"I think maybe I've found a way." I wish my words weren't quite so hesitant.

"Wish I could find a way," he mutters. To himself, really, not to me.

"Pardon?" Is he going to come clean finally?

"Nothing," he says quickly.

"I'm the one who talks to myself around here!" I say.

He laughs too loudly. He's relieved I've brought the conversation around to me.

"So? What is all this?" he begins again.

I affix the last paper to the wall.

"Practice," is all I say. "I've got a lot to do."

He takes the hint. But on his way out, he asks, "How's Candace?"

"Fine. Pretty much as she was the last time you asked." *Get to the point, Uncle Early!*

He stops at the door. "And that guy? Julian?"

"She was trying hard not to like him — I think it has something to do with her mom being pregnant and..." Okay, so my voice is a little angry, a little higher than usual. But does he really have to hurry away down the hallway at a furious pace? Stomp, stomp, then there's a terrific crashing and when I arrive at the top of the stairs, he's at the bottom. The stair railing is actually ripped from the wall. His head is bowed, and I hear a groan.

"Tess!" he calls out.

"Mom!!" I holler at the same time, scrambling down. I almost topple over him and he cringes. I can hear Mom's running steps.

"I think it's my ankle," Early tells her.

I see it now, sticking out in a way ankles aren't meant to. I look away quickly, feeling kind of sick. I'm glad there's no blood: I don't do well with that.

Mom puts a hand on his shoulder. "I'll bring the car right to the door."

She does, driving it over the front lawn, crushing the side of her hydrangea bush. Then both of us help Early to his feet. Or foot rather. I've never heard anyone moan and groan like that. But it's for real. He's dripping with sweat. We help him into the front seat. Mom moves the seat back and the sudden jarring must do something because Uncle Early cries out, then suddenly slumps. From the back seat I can see Mom's hands shaking as she pulls the seat belt over her brother, fastens it, makes certain it's good and tight. She climbs in her side, starts the engine. She takes a deep breath before backing across the yard, then she turns to face the road and steps on the gas.

"I'm glad he held off the passing out until we had him in the car," she says, cutting through a gas station to avoid the cars at a red-light corner.

At the Emergency doors, these guys come out, wearing green stuff. Like on TV, I think. They put Uncle Early on a gurney, wheel him through the doors.

"Do you want to go with him while I park the car?"

"Nope. I'll go with you," I say. "He's out of it. He'll never know."

"Wow. You really aren't happy with him lately, are you?"

"No more than you are."

"What happened today, anyway?" Mom asks as we enter the hospital.

"One minute he's asking about Candace. Next minute he's crashing down the stairs."

"Early's lots of things, but this clumsiness is new." Mom pushes up her sleeves as we approach the desk and mutters, "I guess we have a house guest for a while longer."

The doctor says: "Three weeks, maybe more."

# 27
# Blue Cast

"What's with Early?" Candace waits until we're in the kitchen to speak.

"You mean The Guard."

"I'm still blinking from that flash."

"He's taking photos of everyone who comes through the front door. He just sits on the couch all day, and when he hears a foot on the step, he grabs his camera, and SNAP!"

Candace spies around the open doorway. "He's losing it, just sitting there, foot up, staring at who knows what."

"He won't let anyone write anything on his cast. He growls if you go near him."

"I don't remember Eeyore ever growling in the Pooh books. Too weird." She takes another peek. "Hey!" she says, and she pulls me away from the doorway. "Let's disguise ourselves and come through the front door. We've got to get that bored look off his face!"

"Do you think he looks bored?" Then it's my turn to take a quick peek. He's doing a kid move: his chin rests on the high back of the couch and he's looking out the window. A tired little kid who needs a nap, I think. His slumping shoulders look too adult, though.

"No," I say. "He's found a whole new level to Eeyore's psyche. A low level. Even lower."

"Uncle Gloom'n'Doom," says Candace dourly. "Come on. We'll do something."

We empty the costume trunk. Candace pulls on a floppy old hat, an ugly worn leather coat. It might even have belonged to Uncle Early at some point. A point in time when he had more in common with Tigger than Eeyore.

I pull on an old square-dancing dress. Hard to imagine how this ever found its way into our house. And a multi-coloured clown wig. We sneak out the back door, tiptoe because Early's ears and camera are always waiting.

"I hope no one thinks we're breaking in!" Candace says.

"Not with my goony Uncle Gloom staring out the front window!"

We push towards the door and burst in singing "YMCA." And oh! I wish we hadn't.

Early starts up, and he must wrench his ankle because the look of pain across his face is terrible. He roars, and I swear the sound pushes us right out of the room, because Candace and I are suddenly in the kitchen and I can't even remember how we got there. Candace is crying. "Oh no!" she's saying. "Oh no!" over and over. "We've killed him! He's gonna have a heart attack! I know it!"

Mom's in the doorway.

"We were trying to cheer him up," I say lamely.

"That's just not possible," she says with a voice I've not quite heard before. "He's determined to be the skeleton at the feast!" She turns toward the living room and raises her voice. "Do you need the doctor, Early?"

"No!" he thunders.

Mom raises a brow and returns to the work in her room. Her door actually slams.

Candace's mouth is hanging open. I put a finger under her chin and gently close it.

Then we go to the door and look through. Uncle Early's eyes are closed: a DO NOT DISTURB sign over his nose.

I pull off the clown's wig.

"I'll go now," says Candace. "Out the back door." She piles her costume pieces onto the floor by my wig. I just nod. The house is so quiet after she leaves. Uncle Early hardly seems to breathe. He doesn't even rattle and snore as he used to.

I go upstairs to my room but it's too quiet there, too. Pick up Millicent and go back downstairs to sit in the armchair. Early's turned away from me, but I can see his chest rising and falling, so I know he's still breathing. No heart attack yet.

Millicent sits on my knee and I look at her. I've got to

come up with an entire act for us now, for the show. A week and a half to go. I suppose I could use one of those dialogues from a library book.

Millicent looks around the room. I love the motion of stretching her neck.

"Go ahead," I whisper. "Stretch out your neck."

"Stretch yours!" she whispers back. Not easy to whisper in her voice, I discover.

I keep moving her. Her head looks around…around…over her shoulder. How far can she turn before her body has to move with her? I try it out with my own body.

And with a little hop and a bump from my own thigh, I can make her cross her leg without me touching her. Cool. She can even swing it around a bit, looking casual.

"You're pretty good at this!" she says.

"Thanks."

"Now you've just got to do something about him!" She jerks her head in the direction of Early.

"What do you have in mind?"

She bends over to one side, then the other, leaning forward, scrutinizing him.

"He's gone, isn't he?" she says finally. "That take-it-easy hippy dude he used to be. What's happened?"

"I don't know."

Early moves in his sleep, and we're both still until he settles again.

"I don't know," I repeat.

"Maybe he should be driving a station wagon."

"Uncle Early?" I laugh, but stop quickly. "You think so?"

Millicent cranes her neck, right out this time, looking down over my sleeping uncle. "Oh," she says, her voice hushed. "The man has a...bald spot. That's what that is, isn't it? That shiny bit?"

I look. "Yup. But you're not supposed to point out stuff like that, Mill. It's rude."

"But I see it; it's the truth. Doesn't Mr. Early like the truth?" She straightens up. "I mean, we all have truths to face. How do you think I feel? Waking up in the morning, and knowing I have a wood head? Imagine how *that* feels! Say...do you think he'd want to borrow my wig? I could share. He'd look fine as a redhead, no?"

"Thanks, but no thanks," comes Early's voice from the couch.

I jump. For a moment I think of running from the room, but that would make it worse. What did I think was going to happen? Funny how I got caught up in the conversation and forgot Uncle Early still has ears.

But Millicent presses on. "Well, is it? Is that what's bugging you? You have a bald spot. And that braid thingamajig. It's too much. You know, I'm not exactly a fashion queen. Look at this dress I'm wearing, will you? It's a baby dress for heaven's sake. Maybe you could discuss this with What's-Her-Name with her hand up my back. But really. I like to think I know a few things. And you're no teenager."

I catch a glimpse of Early's face. He looks as if he's just broken his ankle all over again.

"Ssshhhhhh!" I say to Millicent.

She ignores me. "I mean, most guys your age are driving SUVs full of hockey gear for their kids."

"Enough already!"

But Uncle Early doesn't even look at me as he turns on the couch, pain all over his face; he stares at Millicent as he speaks. "Believe me: I never imagined I'd be a balding old guy lying around in my sister's living room."

"Lucky for you, you have a sister," says Millicent quickly. Primly, I think.

Early's quiet for a moment. "Yeah. Lucky," he says. Pauses before going on. "I always wanted to be a crazy guy, an adventurer, someone who lived life as if in a book or a movie. All the exciting bits back to back. Not even time to find the john. Now, I don't even have a place to hang my paintings. Just a blue cast for half my leg to live in and a bag of camera equipment over my shoulder." He grins weakly. "Hey! Maybe we could run away. I'm good at that."

"Nah," Millicent drawls. "You can't go anywhere." She jogs her head in my direction. "And I have to take her along, you know."

"I know." His eyes barely flick in my direction. "I used to think it would be terrible travelling in two. Or three. One's always been the number for me."

"And now?" The question is more from me, but still in Millicent's voice. I can't quite believe she's getting this far into his head.

"Now," he mutters, and rolls onto his back, staring at the ceiling. A pose I've seen too often in the last few days.

"Now, I just don't know. I do know nothing seems right anymore. I feel like I'm a kid, and I've been hiding under the dining room table." His voice drops to a whisper. "No one can see me, safely behind the tablecloth. But the big dinner is over. They've even finished the dishes, all that clanking and chit-chat, and most are gone home."

I think he's finished his speech, though it doesn't seem to be quite the end. And it's not; after a long break, he goes on. "Then somebody comes along and takes off the tablecloth. I have to climb out, and you know, the world's different from how it was when I first went under the table."

He's said a lot. Could I push for more? No. I gather Millicent and leave the room. Go to my own and sit on the edge of the bed. I'm shaking, though I haven't noticed until now. Talk about coming out of hiding and finding the world a different place! I've crawled farther out of that dark place, but the light is shining so brightly in my eyes, I can't see a thing right now.

Mom's working in her room. I knock on her door to let her know I'm leaving for school, and the soft click of computer keys stops. "That's for you." She points to a small box on the bed.

"What is it?"

"A few of your father's things I packed up when you were little. I came across it when we were carrying boxes from the Hole."

I start to open the flaps of the box, but the name written across the cardboard stops me. The letters fill one flap end to end, big red felt pen letters, in a comfortable loose scrawl.

GUMLEY, with the tail of the Y underlining the other letters. "Who wrote this?" I ask.

Mom only needs to glance at it. "Your dad," she says. "He always wrote his name like that." She smiles and goes back to her work. I trace the letters before opening the box. I've never thought to do that with the Y.

On top of everything else in the box is an object wrapped in flannel. I pull it out: a large magnifying glass with a piece of amber-coloured cellophane wrapped around it. Can't imagine why. Next there's a pronged branch, a perfect Y. Tied to the tips of the Y is a black ribbon. Exhibit #2. Then a shirt, summer plaid: orange, red, black and cream. Under that a toy, a train engine, green and gold, and... My heart stops when I see the second toy: weighty, metal, painted with precision and cared for. A motorbike. Did he play with this and dream of riding one someday? I can't touch it. I replace the train and the shirt.

I hold up the magnifying glass, and interrupt Mom. "Why the cellophane?" I ask, looking through the amber.

"It kept the words on the page for him." Mom laughs gently at my confusion. "Your father was mildly dyslexic. He found that the amber colour helped him read."

I had no idea. I hold up the Y branch.

Mom takes it. "When he was about nine or ten, he made this slingshot. He killed a bird with it. He took the elastic off and tied on this ribbon."

When I leave, she still has the branch in her hands. I kiss the top of her head and hurry. I've missed homeroom. I'll give Candace the magnifying glass at lunch.

# 28
# Chickens

*U*ncle Early lives on the couch. Tells Mom that if she brings the laundry to him, he'll be happy to fold it.

"Come on," he says, "tell me about your practising. What do you need to do? What can I help you with?"

"Nothing, really. I need to finish writing a routine...I know! How about you do my school homework for me so I can get at it!"

"Nothin' doin'!" He grins. "What about that routine, though? Bring Miss Milli down here and let's come up with some dialogue."

"I was just going to use a dialogue book," I begin, but Early cuts me off, and I see a spark in him I haven't for a long time.

"No way!" he says. "All the funniest people use their own material!" I think he'd leap up and get Millicent himself if he could.

And I have one of those moments when I suddenly remember what this is all about: getting back up on stage. When I'm practising my funny sentences, even when I was helping Candace to make Millicent, I can and could let myself forget. Now I'm back on the stage, stumbling and wooden, then rushing off, until Uncle Early's voice snaps me back. "Come on," he urges. "You're on stage in a week!"

I leap out of my chair and head up the stairs. "I'll get her," I holler. The loudness of my voice, the abrupt movement – all a plan to scare that thought away. Though, where can it go? It's more than a thought: it's reality. *In one week.*

I sit with Millicent on my lap, and my head begins to clear.

"Any ideas?" Early asks.

"Nothing so far. It seems like so much just to learn how to do this."

"Yeah, your lips are flapping away big time!"

"Thanks! That's what I need to hear!"

"But!" He waggles a finger at my sarcasm. "In spite of the lip movement, I've gotta admit, you have me believing."

"Believing?"

"In Millicent. She's an amazing little being."

"She is," I admit. I'm a little awestruck myself. But there is something else.

"Kinda gets up your nose, doesn't it?" Millicent says, and her head snaps around to look at me.

"Couldn't have said it better myself," I say.

"It's not easy being the straight guy – gal, I mean." Millicent clucks with sympathy. "I know, I know. Tough job and all that. But someone's gotta do it. We can't all be adorable and clever, like me."

"You do tend to take over," I say.

"That's my job!"

I attempt to make her straighten, look proud, cocky even.

"Frank Oz says it took him about ten to fifteen years to move his puppets naturally," Uncle Early says.

"How did you know that's what I was thinking?"

"I'm watching you struggle," he says gently.

I swallow. "Who's Frank Oz?" I whisper.

"One of the people behind the Muppets." He smiles. "And a few other things."

"Ten to fifteen years, huh?"

He nods. "You're doing well, Mally girl. Flapping lips and all." He rests his cast on the coffee table and rubs his hands together. "Well?" He looks at us expectantly, from under the eyebrows that have always been too old for his face, and from his light blue eyes – the colour most likely to lose sight early, he told me once, in a particularly Eeyore mood. But his ears seem to stretch when he's eager, excited about something. I've always loved that look on his face.

I think of another pair of pale blue eyes I've known.

"What do you think Grand would have thought of

Millicent?" I ask.

He waves his hand in the air. "Oh, Grand," he says, as if shooing the thought away.

I have the suspicion that I don't want to hear his answer, but I ask what he means.

"Grand was an old snob really," he says. It's not an answer, though. He picks at his cast, smoothing some bit. He's thinking. "For Grand," he says at last, "being on stage was next to being God. Being a ventriloquist would have been a bit like being runner-up. Grand was not a runner-up kind of person."

"But then," I interrupt, "Grand was never actually on stage, was she?"

"There you go," he says cryptically.

"She did love Edgar Bergen, and his Mortimer Snerd," I point out.

"Ah, but she'd never admit to it!" He shakes his head.

I have the sudden thought that it couldn't have been easy being a child of Grand. I've always thought of her as being so colourful and BIG, but the picture Early shows me is different – one that has room for her own dreams alone.

"What did she think of Mom being an accountant?"

Early laughs then. "It confounded the old gal that all your mother wanted as a child was an abacus."

*Whoa! Now there's a new picture: Mom the rebellious bean counter!*

Early goes on. "I finally had to make her one: seems to me it was of coat-hanger wire and coloured beads."

*Okay: bead counter.*

"It was for her fifth birthday, just before kindergarten. It was pretty much all she played with for the next two years." His face darkens. "I remember my mother was beside herself that the dress and makeup kit she gave Tess sat unused in a corner. Once, Tessie couldn't find her abacus for two days. I think our mother had a hand in that." His eyes narrow.

I remember how when I was little, Grand would bring a trinket for me: a mini tube of lipstick, an odd little evening bag, a cape or pair of shoes, odds and ends for the costume trunk. How I'd looked forward to her visits because of that.

"Hark!" Uncle Early startles me. He cups his hand around his ear and listens. "Is that the sound of tumbling from atop a pedestal?" And his usual laugh. Now, though, I hear a sadness behind the sound. Is it new? Or has it always been there and I haven't heard it before?

Millicent sniffs. "Could be you hear the sound of a chainsaw ripping through the pedestal." She puts her head back and hollers, "Timber!"

"Could be," agrees Early. "Come to think of it..." His voice has a tone of wonder. "She *did* leave you something after all, didn't she?"

"She did?"

He nods thoughtfully. "Would you ever have dreamed Millicent if your wall hadn't been graced with the likes of Charlie McCarthy and Mr. Snerd?"

There's a loud sniff from Millicent. "That picture? The fellow with the humongous nose? And the other with the whatchamacallit stuck in his eye? They were inspiration for *me?*"

"Miss Sneckle, you're in a class of your own," says Uncle Early.

She's about to keep going, but I interrupt her. "Enough..." I say. "Sshhh. He's right, you know. Grand has given me something after all. She didn't really abandon me. Not entirely."

"A sort of cue," adds Uncle Early.

"Huh!" says Millicent. But that's all, and she settles down onto my lap.

"Well," says Uncle Early, "we need a joke to get us started. Didn't Tessie buy you a joke book a few years back?"

"How about this," I say. "Why did the chicken cross the road?"

"Oh no! Not a chicken joke."

"Because she was positive the road came before the egg."

Early just stares. "You made that up!"

"See? That's what happens when I make up stuff," I say. "Try this then: why did the chicken NOT cross the road?"

Early says nothing.

Millicent speaks up. "I know! I know! Because she was afraid of all the lousy jokes that people would tell about her!"

"Ha!" Early's laugh is loud and he slaps his thigh. Then winces in pain. "The possibility of lousy jokes has certainly kept me from doing a few things in my time."

"You can't cross the road because you have a broken ankle," I remind him.

He nods. "That's my excuse at the moment. But I've always been able to find SOME reason not to cross the road."

"What road is it that you want to cross?" The question comes from Millicent.

Early looks vague. "You know, there's always some road you're supposed to cross."

"Maybe...it's a different road."

"Maybe." He doesn't look convinced.

"Are you saying you're a chicken?"

"A chicken who's afraid that if I cross the road, I might not be able to go back."

"Why would you want to?"

Early shrugs. "Might miss something."

"What?"

"I don't know."

"Then why worry about it?"

"Might be something good."

"Maybe the other side of the road is something good. After all, Molly found me on the other side of the road."

"That's not true," says Early. "She found you on her own side of the road. She stumbled over you. Lucky Molly. Now you're going to help her to the other side."

Millicent breaks into sudden song, something like a country tune, mournful and silly. "I was in the middle of the road when you found me. You picked me up and life turned around..."

"Nice twang," says Early. "If I found one of you in the middle of my road, I might be convinced to cross, too. You know" – he leans as close as he can to Millicent – "there are times when I suspect none of this has anything to do with the road: times I think maybe I'm just plain old scared of being a chicken!"

Millicent leans too. "You should be. Unknown territory, pal. Face it: you're a rooster."

"Okay." Early sits back. "Maybe that's what I'm afraid of."

"Come on," says Millicent now. "Let's finish with the chicken-rooster-road stuff. What are you trying to say anyway?"

Uncle Early picks up his unlit pipe from the coffee table, taps the bowl of it in his cupped hand. When he speaks, his words are for me. "Sometimes I forget you're not a little kid anymore. I keep thinking there's things I shouldn't talk about with you." He breathes deeply. "When you were a toddler, and your dad died – when your mom became a widow, and a mom on her own – I kind of ran away." He pauses.

"What do you mean 'kind of'? Did you run away or didn't you? Or don't you even know?" I feel the same way I did with him in the car. But you can't hit a guy in a cast.

He curls in on himself as if I'm holding a branding iron out to him.

"I got an assignment, went to Eastern Europe not even a month later."

"You mean you asked for an assignment," Millicent speaks up. I wish the words had come from my mouth.

Uncle Early looks even smaller. "You're right. I asked them if they had something for me to do, and I bought a ticket that same afternoon. I remember going down to the travel agency. The rain was cold and it was so windy. I remember thinking about your mom, my sister, how even the weather had conspired to add to her grief. I couldn't stand it. Being anywhere near all that pain. I remember climbing aboard the plane, taking my seat. The thought that was in my head as we took off was that I never wanted a family. I never wanted to go through that pain; and I didn't ever want to cause that sort of pain."

"But you seem to be in pain all the time now," I say, and he knows I'm not talking about his ankle.

He's quiet, stares at the cold, dark fireplace. Is he thinking of warm family nights we've shared, or nights when the weather was just as he described moments earlier? Or is he just looking in that direction, not seeing anything, his mind filled with his own pictures of who knows what?

"Yeah," he says finally. "And you're going to be in pain too, if you don't do what you need to." He looks at me directly. "I'm glad you didn't listen to this old guy when I told you to quit."

For Uncle Early that's a big apology.

"After all," he goes on, and he reaches down and pulls a soft knitted slipper from under the couch. He throws it at me, catches my shoulder. "After all, there's no business like shoe business!"

"That's BAD, Uncle Early!" But I laugh just the same.

"You can use it in your act, if you like," he offers, all grandiose.

"Gee, thanks!"

# 29

# Pieces

It's the second week of December and the house is still dark.

"I'll have to take over your job this year," I tell Uncle Early.

He points to the Hole. "The lights used to be in there. In a box on the right shelf."

I find the box, after moving aside eleven paintings. It's under the papier mâché tortoise. "What do you expect us to *do* with all this?"

"All *this* is art," calls Uncle Early from the kitchen table. He's starting to hop around, trips to the fridge mostly.

I set the box of lights on the coffee table as he takes his usual place. I have to rake a few cobwebs from my hair. "So," I begin. "What is Mom going to do about her cello? Have you heard her lately? She's playing Mozart."

Early interrupts with a smile. "You mean, *Twinkle, Twinkle,*

*Little Star. "*

"Ancient folk tunes, whatever, she's playing it. It sounds pretty good, too. Considering."

Early looks serious then. "It does, doesn't it?" He catches sight of Mom in the doorway.

"Tessie!" he calls out. "When are you going to share your music with the rest of the world?"

"Oh, I'm not ready for that!"

"Not true," he says. "You are ready. Maybe it's the world that's not ready for you, Tess."

Mom scoops a too-short piece of hair behind her ear. She turns a bit pink and shakes her head as she goes back to her room.

"Before you go out with those lights do you think you could measure the Hole for me?"

"I could do that." What's he up to?

I find the measuring tape. "Three by four meters."

Then he asks me to fetch paper, pencil and ruler.

Mom brings round the stepladder before she goes out to the store, and then I'm on my own. It takes until lunchtime to edge the roof with the coloured Christmas lights, and when I come in I find that Uncle Early has fallen asleep, papers on chest, pencil in hand.

I see it now: a plan for the Hole. Mom's library. How did he know she wanted a window? And a window seat. "What do you think?" he asks sleepily, coming to, pulling himself up.

"About time I did something for Tessie."

"You *do* do things for Mom."

"Yeah, hang Christmas lights. No, I mean think about what *she* wants. I need another favour."

"What?"

"Can you bring down that box in the spare room? The one with the photos? Please?" Uncle Early pats his cast. "As soon as I'm out of this thing, I'll cut in the window and put up shelves. You can help me paint."

I find the box and set it on the table. Early reaches under a few manila envelopes and folders and pulls out a frame. "Thought Tessie would like this one. In her library." He hands it to me. "It's Tess...and Will."

I've never thought of my father as 'Will,' or of 'Tess and Will.' I touch the glass as if by doing so I can be a part of the happiness that was so plainly between them. *Mom and Dad.* Their arms are wrapped around each other and beside them is a tree as big as a house. White-crested waves ride the ocean behind.

We hear Mom's car pull up to the house, the kitchen door open, her footsteps. "The lights look good," she begins. I hand her the plans, and she looks at them for a moment.

"We thought we'd best get started on it, Tessie," says Uncle Early.

Mom runs her hands over the paper as if seeing the future in her fingertips. "A room of my own," she murmurs.

"Don't know if I'd go that far," says Uncle Early apologetically. "Maybe a space of your own."

She looks at him. "Thanks, bro."

"Mally's helping."

I've been holding the photograph to myself. Now I hand it to her. "We thought maybe this could be on your wall."

I don't know how she's going to react. This is something that's so deep in her, I just can't say. But I'll take the chance.

"Oh," is all she says at first, holding the photo in both hands, her fingers spread over the back of the frame. Then: "I remember that day." She speaks softly, steps into the Hole and slowly places the photo on a hook that used to hold skates. Sure we can see her standing there, but it does feel as if she's stepped away, into her own place. Not too far away, though.

I have another piece for my collage," says Candace.

"What is it?"

"I don't know," she says. "Come over and we'll figure it out."

Sounds mysterious. "I have a couple of things," I tell her.

"Good," she says. "You can put them on first."

I put my offerings in a large envelope, and go over. Sure enough, the collage is mostly unchanged except for the magnifying glass. "Here," and I pull the cardboard flap from my envelope.

Candace takes it, holds it up.

"It's how my dad felt about our name," I explain. Just as I did, Candace traces the red letters with her finger, ending with the flourishing Y.

"How about here?" She places it at the end of the trail of nails, tilted to a jaunty angle.

"Oh, yes." I nod approval. Funny, I never thought the *Gumley* moniker would cause me to feel anything other than...chagrin.

And my final piece. I reach into the envelope and pull it out, hand it to her. She holds the sprig of dried chamomile to her nose and breathes in. One of the faded yellow flowers comes away and she rolls it in her fingertips. Another deep breath of the scent. Then she sort of stops; she's still. And in a curious voice, she says, "It *is* Uncle Early." So both of us are surprised.

"How did you...?" I begin, but her answer is so quick she overtakes my words.

"I've just somehow always known."

So here we are, all keeping secret about the same thing.

"We're not supposed to know."

"No?" she says then. She holds the sprig here and there on her collage, trying to find the right place. "You've always admired his independence, his ability to just take off whenever he wanted. I couldn't ask you about him."

So Grand's not the only person I've had on a pedestal. What did Early say? *'They always topple.'*

I pick up the two halves of the wooden spool that Avery gave to Candace. "What about this?"

She holds them and thinks. Then she takes the glue gun and affixes one of the pieces to the board, on its side. She writes with a felt pen 'HUNNY' and places the bit of burst balloon beside it. "Eeyore's birthday present," she says. Close by, she sets the other half of spool upright, and tucks the sprig of chamomile into the half hole in the top. "For Eeyore's other birth-day," she says with a sad smile.

After awhile, I ask her to tell me about her collage piece. "What's that about?"

When she speaks, there's still sadness to her, but a settled sort of sadness. "My mother was going on and on about something the other night. That same old thing she talks about: how a person cuts themselves off when they see themselves in only one way. At first, I thought she was talking about me, and that 'your heart can be an elastic blah-blah-blah,' but then I realized it was different, and I asked her: 'are you talking about my father?' She looked really surprised when I asked her, as if she hadn't thought of it that way. 'Yes, I think I am.' So I just asked her about him – why he didn't stick around."

"And what did she say?"

Candace gives a snaggly sort of laugh. "He's an artist. He didn't think he could be anything else, was how he explained it to Mom. Seems to me," she goes on thoughtfully, "that an artist needs to be more than just an artist if they're going to be an artist at all." Then she looks apologetic. "You know what I mean?"

"I think so." Then, slyly, I add, "Maybe an artist can even be a sister."

She doesn't answer that, but goes over to her worktable and takes a paintbrush from one of the cans she's nailed to the wall. First, she dips it in thick black paint, and paints a heavy circle on the far and bare side of the collage. Then more hot glue, and she sets the brush in the middle of the circle.

I'm thinking of Avery suddenly. Her place in this. "Your mom always stuck around," I say.

"She had to," is Candace's quick response, but then she's quiet.

"I think she chose to," I say.

Then I tell her what Avery told me, how the baby felt like a gift — a gift no one wanted to share with her.

"I wonder if that's how she felt about me, too," says Candace.

## 30

# Dress Rehearsal

ere." Mom stands in my doorway, with something in her arms hidden under a blanket.

I open the door wide for her, and she sets it on the bed. I pull off the blanket. Under it is an old suitcase, oxblood red, leather, with big brass clasps and a heavy handle.

"It was Grand's, in her locker with the cello. I wasn't sure what to do with it. Look." After a brief struggle with the clasps she opens it. Inside, she's made a foam bed for Millicent, with extra padding for her head, soft flannel to cover her face. "You can still use this pocket." She shows me how to get at it behind the foam. "For props, extra clothes." She pulls out a little garment and hands it to me. "I thought maybe Millicent could use some funky little overalls."

It takes me a minute to recognize the fabric: Grand's old plaid robe. And Mom used the belt to make the shoulder straps.

Already my fingers are slipping off the red dress and I'm pulling on the overalls. Mom hands me a child's bright T-shirt.

I'll give the dress back to Avery.

"This is it," I breathe to Millicent as I straighten the overalls, tuck in the shirt. I shiver.

"Let's journey on, sister," she says to me.

I put her into the suitcase, tuck the flannel over her face, and close the case.

"Ready, Molly?" Mom calls up the stairs.

I pick up the suitcase and switch off the light. Downstairs, Mom hands me my coat. She's wrapped a scarf around her own neck, made with red and silver threads, and her going-out purse is slung over a shoulder.

"You're not coming?" I ask. Mom comes to everything.

"I'll be there when you perform. Tonight, I'm going to another performance."

"Your cell phone?" I point it out to her, on the little table in the entrance hall.

"I won't need my phone tonight," she says. "I'm going to a cello recital. 'Intimate' it's called, which means maybe twenty people in a room of one of those big old Granville Street mansions. If my phone rings they'll use my guts to make the next set of strings!"

I have to grin with her. "No, they won't. Too messy."

"Actually," she says, "I'm hoping to meet a Mrs. Rumpf and beg her to teach me how to get a real sound from that thing."

"Good luck!" I wish her.

"Before you break a leg," she warns, "remember that the couch is already occupied."

Candace takes the suitcase from me. "This is cool." Inside the house, she asks, "May I?" and opens it without waiting for my answer. "Millicent looks great. The overalls are perfect!" She smiles over her creation before snapping closed the lid.

Candace pulls on a heavy wool sweater and goes through a basket of knit stuff looking for gloves. "We can walk to school, I told Mom. She was worried about us going by ourselves. But she's not feeling well. Kinda crampy, she says."

"Candace?" Avery's voice comes from the upstairs. Though it doesn't really sound like Avery. Kind of wavery. Like an old person's.

"Mom?" Candace freezes in the act of pulling on a glove.

No answer. "Mom?" she calls out again. She begins to take off the glove.

I put down the suitcase as she pushes me aside and heads up the stairs. "MOM!" she calls out, her voice sharp. I follow. I'm just behind Candace as she pushes open the door to her mother's workroom.

Avery is on her hands and knees. My first thought is that she's lost something on the floor and is looking for it. But her face says it's not that. Her face is ghost white, her eyes are big. Scared. The fear makes her features almost unrecognizable, just like her voice.

"Something's wrong," she says now. "I don't know what." But of course she knows, and we do too: the baby.

Avery's wearing the maternity pants that she's spent the last month in, a gingerbread colour. I can see the elastic panel that stretches over her belly; it always makes me feel strange to see it. And I can see the crotch of her pants, wet.

"Your water's broken?" asks Candace. *Sounding like a* TV *character*, is my first thought. No, there's that book she read; she learned a few things, I guess.

"I don't know," Avery says again. "I don't remember it being like this." Her voice trembles. "And this is early...oh!" she says all at once, and her face contorts. She lowers herself onto her elbows – looks like a horse struggling to get to its feet – and moans.

"A contraction?" Candace's voice is so cool. *Clinical*. But then she turns to me and her face colour matches her mom's. She pulls on my sleeve, pulls me out of the room. Around the corner, her voice is different. "What do we do *now?*"

"I thought you read that book."

But Candace is starting to shiver. "You know, mice eat books," she says senselessly.

"Yeah." *Where is she going with this?*

"In places like attics. Places like my new room."

"Maybe," I offer. *Do we really have time for this?* I push down the panic rising in me. Just around the corner, Avery's having her baby.

"I've heard mice," Candace continues. "In the walls up there. I'm sure of it. Little scratchy sounds."

"Well, move back into the house, then."

She shakes her head vigorously and the motion travels unbidden through the rest of her body. There's a moan from Avery.

"They're supposed to be farther apart," she says in a gasping sort of way.

We move back to the doorway to hear her words; it's not easy to understand.

"The contractions," she says. She doesn't look at us. In fact, I wonder if she knows we're anywhere near her.

"That's right," says Candace, in a leap-to-it voice. "We're supposed to be timing the contractions."

"All the time!" The words are pushed from Avery's gut. "They don't stop!" The mixture of anger and fear in her voice scares me.

"We're supposed to find out how far apart the contractions are, and how long they last," Candace goes on. "Watch your second hand," she tells me, pointing to my watch. She's never worn one.

I do, but when I glance at my wrist again, the second hand looks as if it's in the same place. So much more than a minute seems to have passed though. Can it possibly be two? Feels like an hour.

Then Avery is still. Her eyes stay closed. Sweat drips down the opening at the neck of her shirt. For a second, I think she's going to fall asleep. There's a limpness to her. Do women still die in childbirth?

*Come on, Molly! Don't think like that!*

Where *is* Candace?

I hear running water from the bathroom.

Candace hollers something about hot water. Reminds me of the TV thing again.

"That's *boiling* water you're supposed to get, and I don't think they do that any more!" I yell back. *Would it help if I slapped her face? Nah, that's a* TV *thing, too.*

I look back at Avery. She's starting to stir again, her face twisting into a grimace. I think of the woman who came and talked to some of the students about sex and family planning.

Really, if she'd had a videotape of Avery at this very moment, she'd never have had to give that talk: no one who saw this would want to risk it.

Some bit of this thought must show on my face, because when Candace returns from the bathroom, she looks at me with suspicion. "What?! What's so funny?"

"Not funny," I say. "I'll tell you another time."

But too late — she's furious. "What are you laughing at?" Then she starts to cry. "My mom's dying in there, Molly. I know it. Something's not right. It's not supposed to be like this."

I don't tell her the thought crossed my mind moments before. I think of Mom, alone, travelling into town, with no phone. Uncle Early's probably snoozing on the couch, probably unplugged the phone as he does sometimes.

"We've got to do something," Candace says in a tearful whisper.

"All right," I say slowly. In a drawl. So I can think about it. The slowdown works. An answer comes. *Aha! Millicent. You are so right.*

"Call 911."

"Of course!" Candace's words are filled with relief, and she runs to get the phone.

Even as I push the buttons, Avery is going into another...contraction. I try out the word in my head.

"Fire, police, ambulance?" the operator asks.

"Ambulance." I can hear the tremble in my voice. I clear my throat.

Then she asks what's happening, and I tell her, looking at Avery, whose eyes are blurry with pain.

"Address?" asks the operator. Her voice is smooth, calm. Even the sound of her breathing calms me. She begins to give me directions.

"We need a clean surface." I relay the instruction to Candace. She fetches a blanket, and I help her spread it.

"Pants off." There's no time for embarrassment.

We aren't going to be able to get those pants off. Avery is shivering, and no part of her body is listening to her anymore, let alone to us. But she does manage to reach into a drawer in the sewing table, and pull out a pair of shears. She glances at Candace.

Candace, I see, can't move. So Avery hands the scissors to me and I pass the phone to Candace. My hands are shaking as I put the blades to the fabric and cut through that elastic gingerbread. The fabric falls to the floor. The sudden whiteness of her skin startles me. But not as much as the red lines scribbled and stretched all over her belly. She shudders, sways as the cold air hits her.

"Where's another blanket?" I ask Candace, and she finally moves to leave the room. The operator hears.

"Good thinking," she says. "Do keep her warm. With a rapid birth, she may feel like throwing up. Keep a bowl handy..." But she's too late. Avery is retching, and then the smell of vomit fills the room. The odor stops Candace at the door, and she looks suddenly confused.

I grab the blanket from her. "Get a washcloth, a towel."

I try not to breathe deeply as I wash Avery's face, smooth her hair from her face, smooth the knots of lines that have gathered on her forehead. She looks so dismayed.

"You're going to be all right," I whisper. Her eyes meet mine, and I see such fear in hers before they close.

Outside I hear December wind, and inside I suddenly feel as if Avery's slipping away. "Avery?" I whisper.

The operator is calling for me, I realize. "You need to tell me what you can see. Does she feel like pushing?"

"She doesn't seem to," I answer. Avery is lying on her back, knees up, eyes still closed.

"The contractions seem to have stopped. Or slowed," I tell the operator. Avery's stillness is scaring me. I don't say anything about that.

"If you can see the head, it sounds like time to push." Do I imagine it, or is there just a hint of nerves in the operator's voice? "She has no urge to push?" she questions again. This time I ask Avery.

She shakes her head, a vehement shake, and a convulsive sob comes from her.

"She's going to have to..."

Candace's voice cuts off the operator's words. "Look!" she says. "The head. I think I can see the head!"

I work to fight the panic rising in me, and Avery calls out, again with fear. This time with something new: a dreadful terror, I think.

I can't let her hear the same in my voice. "The ambulance is going to be here in a minute..."

Avery's thighs are going into spasm. I've never seen the head of a baby about to be born, but I'm pretty sure that's what it is we're looking at. My eyes prickle with tears.

I think she's holding her breath now; she's fighting. I touch her arm. "You've got to push, Avery. You do. Now."

*Where* is that ambulance?

What was it that book of Candace's said? That strange sentence…oh, yes…*your child is on the other side of your pain.* As I think of those words, an image comes to me. Not an image, exactly; more like a sensation. Sort of like the sensation of fear I'd felt on the high school stage that first time, as if I was seeing through into a tunnel, a menacing tunnel. Maybe it's like that. "You have to tunnel through," I tell Avery. "Through to the other side, and she'll be there."

Avery seems to be listening. Or maybe it's just that the contraction is passing. Her breathing evens.

"It'll be okay," I say.

Another contraction begins. Her breathing grows ragged. She is pushing finally. The sound that comes from her almost makes me pull away. I force myself to stay, even as the animal sound dies away, only to begin again, a thick cry, a sound of something freed.

Through the window, there comes the red flashing lights of an ambulance. There are blue lights, too. Candace's feet pound down the stairs to let them in. The paramedics are in the room in seconds, followed by a policewoman.

At first they seem to think they're going to prepare Avery for the hospital, but one quickly says, no, this baby's going to be born right here.

A paramedic moves in beside me. "You're almost there…another push." But there's another, then another, and then, suddenly there's the back of the baby's head, red and dark; another moment, and a shoulder. And suddenly she slips out with a final great push from Avery, who is crying — though it might be laughter, I'm not sure. The paramedic puts the baby on Avery's belly, and she holds her, bloody and wrinkled, and with such a big head, such little feet. There's a cord — I can't remember the word for it, though I know I've heard it — and it's rubbery looking, and coiled like an old-fashioned phone cord. It connects the two of them, mother and baby. The other paramedic takes a blanket from some sort of bag she has, and wraps it over them. Candace is in tears, with an arm round her mom. I step back, out of the light, into a darkened corner, and I breathe deeply. I don't realize that I am shivering until the paramedic wraps a blanket around me, too, and pushes me gently into a chair.

They work with Avery and the baby, prepare to take them to the hospital. "Probably just for the night." The words they speak flow over me. I don't pay much attention, though I catch a few.

"Come. I'll take you home." The policewoman's voice is soft and she touches my shoulder. "Is that yours?" She points to Millicent's suitcase waiting in the entrance hall.

"That's mine," I say and wrap my arms around it and follow her to the car.

# 31

# Out In the World

S o?" Uncle Early pulls himself upright on the couch. He's been dozing obviously. "How was it?" he asks groggily.

I set down my suitcase. "How was what?" How can he possibly know what I've been doing tonight?

He looks startled. "The dress rehearsal." He speaks as if he's suddenly fearful that he might be losing his mind.

"The dress rehearsal," I repeat.

I lean against the arm of the chair. "I didn't go," I say, feeling numb all at once.

I'd thought so much depended on that rehearsal, hadn't I?

I begin to laugh, a nervous laugh, high and twittery, like a little girl's. Then it explodes into a real laugh and all at once I'm crying. Uncle Early pushes himself up from the couch, and heaves himself to his feet. He beckons to me, and I move into his arms for the hug I know so well. "I'm okay," I blubber. "Nothing wrong. It's just..." Just what? I can't think.

He releases me, leans on the crutch he keeps by the couch. I push him gently back to the couch. "Sit," I tell him. I realize I'm grinning like an idiot at him. He smiles somewhat uncertainly, at me.

"What did happen tonight?"

"The most wonderful thing," I begin.

His eyes slide to the suitcase.

"No," I say. "Not that. The baby was born. And Candace and I were there. She was born at home. She came suddenly."

"She?" he asks.

"It's a girl. Avery hasn't chosen a name yet." The words burst out, want to tumble over each other. Suddenly the earlier part of the evening seems fantastic, unbelievable, and the only way I can make it believable is to go over every detail. But he interrupts me.

"The baby is...here?"

"Tonight, just when we were getting ready to go to school for the rehearsal, Avery went into labour. And we called 911."

Early has a sick look on his face and he's struggling to stand again. He's kind of scaring me, he's so pale. One medical emergency is enough for the night, thanks. "Are you all right?" It occurs to me that I have absolutely no idea what time it is. Could be eight in the evening, or three the next morning for all I know.

He doesn't answer my question. He asks one of his own. "Was she all right?"

"The baby?"

"Avery."

"It all happened so fast."

He looks away, seems to be chewing his bottom lip, and then my uncle, my big, tough uncle is crying. Oh not sobbing, or anything like that, but a tear, followed by another, is moving down his cheek into his beard.

"She's okay," I whisper. *Come on, Uncle Early. You knew this was going to happen. Don't freak me out like this.* "The baby, and Candace...everything went well. The paramedic said there were no complications. They're spending the night at the hospital; they'll probably be home tomorrow." My voice drifts off.

I can't think what else to say to him. Mom has a book called a descriptionary: it's like a dictionary, but backwards — the description or definition of the word, then the word. I need one of those now.

"I've reached the place where the road narrows, Mally, and I can see what's on the other side," he says. "Problem is, the crosswalk was a ways back and...well, like I told you before, I was afraid to cross. Now it's too late. I'm just a scared old man, Mally, a scared old man who never wanted to live as his mother did. She always lived with her own dream and ignored all the loving people around her. I always thought that if I were going to live with a dream, I'd live on my own. That way, nobody'd be hurt."

"But you were the person who told me nobody can do things on their own."

"Sometimes you know things with your head, sometimes with your heart, and sometimes it's hard to convince one to follow the other. I thought I'd just pass on to you what I couldn't do myself."

"So, what was the dream, Uncle Early?" I ask.

He looks perplexed for a moment, as if he needs to remember.

"Freedom, I think it was. Just me and my camera, going where we wanted. Never having to answer to anybody."

The opening of the front door stops him.

"Mom."

"You're still awake!" Her first words.

So it must be late then.

She hangs up her coat. For the hour, there's a lightness in her step, a shine in her eyes. "What a wonderful evening. And Mrs. Rumpf said she'd see me in the New Year!" She pulls off her scarf and tugs at an earring.

"Mom, Avery had the baby," I say. She stops moving, one earring in hand, one still dangling from an ear.

"Oh," she says, "then it's out in the world now." She removes the second earring.

"It's a girl," says Uncle Early.

Mom stares at him. He looks away, but still Mom stares.

"What?" he blusters. Sometimes I can imagine just how they were as kids living in the same house.

"A daughter," says Mom slowly. "Congratulations."

Early has a look on his face, a look as if he'd like to be able to walk out of our house right NOW. Mom won't take her eyes off him, and her eyes are full of reproach.

"What are you going to do, Early?"

"Do?" he says. He looks at me, one of those 'significant' looks, trying to remind Mom.

"I know, too," I say.

"You know?" He's not trying to stand; now he's pushing himself back into the cushions of the couch as if he'd like to disappear.

"You told me," I tell him.

"Me?"

"Yeah, in lots of ways. Ways I didn't see at first, but when you ran away, I figured it had to be something big."

My uncle hangs his head. "I'm sorry, Mally," he says. "Can you forgive an old fool?"

Mom interrupts. "Maybe that's something you have to ask someone else as well. Someone who cares so much for you." Mom's voice is sad. "Why don't you come out from under your rock and look at what the world has to offer? Stop running, brother."

"It's too late." Early repeats his words to me.

"You can't make that decision for others."

Mom turns to go up the stairs. She does look tired now. She puts an arm around my shoulders. "Tell me all about it in the morning, Mol o'mine. Get some sleep; tomorrow is another big day for you. I expect missing the rehearsal was a good rest for Millicent; she's been working hard lately!" She gives me a little hug.

But I'm awake for a while. I never do hear Uncle Early preparing for bed. I don't know how long he stays up into that night — his first as a father. My head is filled with other mysteries of life. Not just my own.

## 32

# Ginger Fuzz

The sun is higher than it should be. The house is quieter.

For the briefest of moments I lie in bed. Feels like Saturday. Something's come to an end; that much I remember. I snuggle deeper under the quilt, revel in the warmth, the flannel softness.

It washes over me. Candace's sister. "Out in the world," is how Mom puts it. But while Avery's pregnancy has come to an end, there are now many beginnings.

Early. Is a father. Candace, a sister. Avery, a mother all over again. Mom and I are Aunt and Cousin. *Cousin.*

And this is the day of the variety show.

I peek out the curtains. Lately when I get up for school, it's quite dark.

Then I clue in. It's late. Mom's already left for a meeting. She must have figured that I needed more sleep.

Downstairs, the couch is empty, Early's blankets folded neatly at the end, and I can hear his voice, soft on the phone. "No, no," he's saying. "I don't want to awaken her, I just want to know that she's all right. And...the baby." He listens for a moment, then, "Good, good. I'll see them when they're home. Thank you ever so much." I can hear as he replaces the receiver and waits before gathering his crutch. Standing takes time. He looks a bit embarrassed as he comes around the corner.

"Mally," he says, still in his soft voice. Something's changed in him. He seems to have slowed. Inside. "Well," he says, sits in the armchair, looks out of place.

"I'm trying to think of how to describe you," I tell him, "and I'm not sure what to say. Even Millicent wouldn't know."

He handles his crutch. "Remember I told you about me being under that table for so long, and how when I come out, everyone's gone and the world is different."

"I remember."

"It seems," he says, "that I forgot to look on the tabletop. It seems that someone has left a full dinner plate. For me. And it's like the dinner in *Where the Wild Things Are*. The food is still warm. After all my wanderings and worries. It's an amazing thing, Mally girl." He shakes his head in wonder. "I don't know what life will be like from this point on. I've never been so unsure of my direction. And it's never mattered less. Something just feels right, that's all."

"What are you going to write on the Bug?" I ask.

He laughs. "There's always that, isn't there. Hmm." He ponders for a minute. "How about 'cross the street'? Or maybe just 'follow your chicken.'"

"See?" I say. "You're still crazy."

"I am, aren't I?" He looks pleased with my words. "Still crazy after all these years." He looks at the clock planted in the brickwork over the fireplace. "You're late," he says.

It's almost ten o'clock. I have a quick bowl of cereal with too much brown sugar, then change from pajamas to jeans. Millicent's case is on the floor by my bed where I left it last night. I have an urge to open it, to touch her face as if for strength to get through this day. I do rest my hand on the handle for a second. "I'll see you later," I whisper. "Tonight."

*Tonight,* I think on the way to school. But tonight was supposed to be last night; the dress rehearsal was supposed to come first. The dress rehearsal was going to be the life-saving ring for me to catch. Now I feel as if I am clutching at a life ring, with no rope attached to it.

"There you are!" It's as if Julian's been waiting for me, he's so close to the door when I step into the school. The hall swells with between-classes rush. "Ms. Tanaka's so freaked. She's already talked to me about having *my* act prepared to go on tonight. Where were you last night?"

I begin to say something about Candace, but he cuts me off. "You are going on tonight, aren't you?"

I notice that there's something odd about his shirt: the buttons start in the wrong hole. And I have the feeling that if I pointed this out, it would bother him. He's just not his usual laid-back self.

"I can't go on," he says.

"Why not?" I ask. *Don't tell me stage fright.*

He glances around as if the drama teacher will pounce on him from inside some locker. "I don't *have* an act," he whispers.

"Of course you have an act! You're the backup." You can never accuse me of being laid back.

"I didn't think you'd really need a backup," he says.

Why can't I have that sort of faith in myself?

I take a deep breath. "How did last night go?"

"Pretty much a mess. Ms. Tanaka kept saying that a bad dress rehearsal means a good performance. But she said it so many times it was hard to believe. Then you didn't show up, and she started to lose it." His voice drifts off suddenly. "What happened to you anyway?"

The knot in my gut loosens suddenly. "Candace's sister was born."

His eyes widen.

"At her house," I add.

"Wow!" is all he can say. "Wow." He takes that in.

But he's not quite finished with me, though the hallway's been empty for minutes. "So? If I see Ms. Tanaka, what do I tell her?"

"I'll go and find her myself," I say.

He seems relieved.

"All right!" he whoops, and bounds away. Then stops. So suddenly I can almost hear the cartoon sound effects. "What do you give to a baby?"

"I don't know."

"Hmm. I'll think of something." He whistles down the hallway.

He will, too.

I start out to find the drama teacher, with that knot in my gut tied tight again.

Before third period, I find her outside her class. She's wearing all black. Even coloured her hair. She doesn't say anything at first, just looks at me with that question she had the first day of school. Finally, she speaks. "Are you able to do this?"

She wants me to say 'yes.' A bold, confident yes. 'Think Positive' and all that.

Even saying 'no' would be easier than what I have to say. "I won't know until I get up there."

She blinks. "Right. Of course. True." She nods. "Sometimes you don't know until the moment is there. I do know what that's like."

I suddenly want to ask. "Ms. Tanaka — what happened in New York?"

She pauses. "Nothing very dramatic. Pun intended." A little chuckle. Then: "I'm not sure I've ever come to terms with it really. Do you know that everyone in my family is a performer?"

I nod.

"My sister is a musician, my mother was a dancer — she teaches now, but she doesn't like to teach. My great uncle and aunt were in the circus and so on. And seven years ago, there I was, in New York, with a small but steady role, living in a funky little apartment I was lucky to have, and one morning I woke up and..." She looks as if she's afraid I might not believe her. "And I didn't want it anymore. It was as if something was turned off in me, some current that had been running for years, suddenly gone. I felt hollow. But not in a bad way. Just in a fillable sort of way. So when the run of the play was over, I packed up and went back to university. Mostly because that's what all my friends had done while I'd been away back east. I ended up with an education degree. Now here I am. Sometimes I'm not sure why. It's kind of scary when something just goes." Her story ends. "Now, my question: where were you last night?"

I tell her.

"Congratulations," she says, and gives my forearm a curious little squeeze — of hope? for luck? — before leaving.

There's a message on the answering machine when I get home. Candace's voice. "Molly! We're home. Come and see my amazing sister!"

So Avery still hasn't chosen a name.

Uncle Early hands me a package: a letter in an envelope addressed to Avery, and what feels like a book wrapped in paper. "I'll give it to her," I promise.

Avery is sitting on the couch, surrounded by pillows, the baby asleep on her belly. I can't believe her belly is still so huge; looks like another baby's in there. The public health nurse is preparing to leave. "Call me with any questions," she says.

"We had questions for you last night," I say cheekily. "Where were you then?"

"Out having dinner with my boyfriend, and yes, the thought kept coming to me that I was supposed to be somewhere else!" She grins. "You must be the midwife friend! Fine work, from what I hear." She's on her way.

Avery smiles as she takes Uncle Early's package, but she puts it to one side, unopened, as the baby stirs and turns her head toward Avery. She opens and closes her lips, pushing her tongue against her upper lip. Her head bobs.

"What's she doing?" I whisper.

"She's rooting," answers Avery. "She wants to nurse." Avery opens her robe and the baby latches on greedily. It all seems just right.

I realize I'm grinning at Avery, pretty much like an idiot. She looks back at me and chuckles, and suddenly we're both blinking tears, wherever they come from.

"You were brave last night, Molly. You told me something I needed to hear."

"You probably knew it already, though," I say, feeling embarrassed, and trying to remember exactly what it was I'd said.

"We all know all sorts of things, but sometimes we need to be reminded by another."

We listen to the sound of the baby suckling, a slurpy contented sound.

"Look at her," says Avery, and she moves so that I can see the baby's face. Her skin is clear, her hair a ginger fuzz. She stops suckling and turns to me. She opens her eyes and I look into them, a deep grey-blue, and I see that there's really not much new to her after all: she knows everything, it seems to me. She knows about fear, and journeying. If I asked her about my questions and about how I felt when I finally touched my Millicent's head, I have the feeling she could tell me all about that. She turns back to Avery as I touch *her* fuzzy warm head, and I feel hope.

## 33
# Hey!

*M*om's made pizza for an early supper – big chunks of feta and fresh tomato slices, my favourites. She doesn't say much, doesn't ask anything, just keeps looking at me, her eyes warm and open, letting me know she's there if I want her, and I'm glad for that. Then it's time to go.

I pick up the suitcase, hold it close, and whisper, "Tonight it's me and you, Millicent Sneckle."

*T*here are still six stairs up to the stage – but I'm at the first, and I haven't thrown up, so that's good...so far. I grip the handle of the suitcase even tighter and try to push away the numbers that accompany my footfalls. Two...three...four. When I reach the top I have to take a deep breath. It's the thought of the audience *out there,* and the sound of waiting. *I want to run away, far, far, far away. Away under the exit sign in the far corner.*

But something calls to me, a soft 'hey!' from the case in my hand. My breathing begins to even. I set the case on the stool. "We're on." But the clasps stick.

*It can't be.* Deep breath. Steady.

Try again. Inside me, the pieces I've so carefully mended are straining: the mortar, the vines, tears, laughter – all that has come to hold them together – it threatens to burst.

I close my eyes, and I can see through the suitcase, can see Millicent's eyes, her smile. After all, the case is only leather, cardboard, thin pieces of metal.

Third try lucky? *No.*

"I guess she doesn't want to play today," I say aloud, and the audience does laugh but it's a holding-back laugh. They're waiting for Millicent, too. I put my thumbs to the clasps, close my eyes – *Millicent, I need you to be here* – and I push. I can't do this on my own. Not yet, anyway. For now, Millicent is a part of who I am.

I try again, and the clasps click.

"Thank you," I breathe.

"Oooo," groans Millicent. "I'm stiff as a board. Can't move I've been stuck in here so long!" There's a terrible creaking sound as she sits up. "Had you all poopin' in your chairs, didn't I? Ha!!"

The audience laugh makes the floorboards sing under my feet.

"Especially you!" She swings round to me, peers at me, then back to the audience. "Oh, maybe not," she drawls.

"Maybe she was hoping I'd be in there forever and she'd have the place to herself."

"Nope – don't want it." *Did that just come out of my mouth?* "Without you, I'm nothing!" I add.

"Hey! That's my line!" she snaps. "But I'll let you have it!"

"What's my line?" I ask.

"They're all a part: my line, your line, their line." Millicent bobs her head at the audience. "Everyone does their bit, and it becomes something bigger. It's like a roomful of people laughing." And Millicent breaks off to imitate a series of laughs: a haw, a hee, tee-hee, a BELLOW. Her body contorts with each and I have to catch her from falling backwards, and almost wrestle her back into a sitting position. Then she's off again, legs and arms in the air, chortling, guffawing, giggling. Only when the entire audience has joined in, does she stop, abruptly. "Ha! See? The laugh grew so big, I bet you forgot what we were laughing about!"

"What were we laughing about?" I ask.

"I dunno." Her head sinks as I raise her body with my knee: a shrug. And the laughter doesn't stop.

So Millicent takes the show. She doesn't steal it, but she does take it to a place I couldn't, not by myself. She's off and running with some joke about a woodpecker, those birds being a special fear of hers, of course, and inside me there's a shift. Nothing tectonic, but a shift. Maybe just all those pieces settling in together.

Then we're flying. We have wings. The sandbags have fallen from our balloon, and we've burst through the roof, we're riding atop clouds of laughter. Free. And it's good. Solid good.

## 34

# Wanna Dance?

hen it's over and the performers and the audience is singing *Auld Lang Syne*.

"You and me, we did it," I whisper to Millicent.

The audience surges forward. I see Candace heading my way as the other performers are hustled off stage by family and friends. I'm to meet Mom at the car.

I hear my name called. It's Julian, and I can hardly see his face behind flowers.

"Too many," I protest.

"But there are two of you!"

I take two blooms, tuck one in Millicent's overalls and the other behind my ear. The rest I hand to Candace. She ducks her head to bury her nose in the blooms and when she looks up again, she's a rather bright shade of red. She flashes me a sheepish smile and then a less-so one for Julian. Julian beams.

"I'll see you two later," I say, laughing. I move just offstage to fetch Millicent's suitcase from where I'd left it. As I pick it up, one of the back curtains brushes my face, a soft touch. Remember when I thought of them as the lungs? My arms wrap around the old suitcase and I stand, breathe in the air. I'm here, aren't I? Backstage. Onstage. I've done it, Grand. In my own different way.

"Molly?" The voice is soft, hesitant. Shy. Although he's smiled and nodded at me since the opening night fiasco, he hasn't actually spoken to me. I turn around.

Millicent speaks before I do. "You!" she says cheerily. "You're gonna talk to *her* again? After she almost threw up on your shoes?"

Caleb laughs.

"Well, don't say I didn't warn ya!" says Millicent, and then I turn her away.

"Don't worry. I think the risk is past." I hesitate. "Wanna dance?"

He looks over to where Ms. Tanaka is moving stuff around on the far side of the stage.

"Later," he says with a grin. "But yes." From the doorway he turns back, gives that head-duck motion. I wonder about his patience during all the weeks that have passed.

I tuck Millicent into her case and jam an edge of the foam into the clasps so there's not a chance they'll stick again.

Ms. Tanaka nears, sits on a table that leaves her feet dangling in the air. "You," she says, "were amazing! If it wasn't your night – and it is! – I'd tell you what happened to me while you were onstage. But I'll tell you another time." She hops off the table and gives me a hug.

"What?" I ask. "I want to know."

"I'll tell you this much: *now* I know why I'm here!" She gives a brief sequence of dance steps. "I *love* being a teacher!"

## 35
# On Board

It's going to be hours before I can sleep. Mom and Early and I have been up talking around the table with Millicent propped in the middle, but Early's gone to the porch for a now-rare smoke of his pipe. I remember that I have a packet for him, from Avery. Candace gave it to me as I left for home.

Are his hands trembling as he takes it?

I hope he doesn't wait to open it. He doesn't. Maybe he knows I've had enough of adult secrets. Or maybe he just can't wait himself.

He laughs, a happy rolling laugh let free. He holds the gift out for me: a name book and a Baby On Board sticker.

"Does this mean you're going to take all those old stickers off the Bug?" I ask.

He shakes his head. "No need to do that. There's still freedom and peace in the world. It's just in different spaces than I'd thought. After all, there's no other way you'd want a baby on board!"

I sit close to him and he opens his blanket as if it's a wing and gathers me in. "Will you help me, Mally girl? Handle these crutches down the sidewalk? I'd like to see my daughter before her first full day comes to a close."

I help my uncle stand, fetch him a warmer coat. We make our way down the steps, the street. Halfway, we stop to rest. He leans on his crutches and against my shoulder, and we watch as the wind pushes clouds and the moon pulls from behind, full and bright enough to throw shadows at us.

# Alison Acheson

Alison Acheson has published a previous teen novel, *Mud Girl,* which was a finalist for Canadian Library Association's Young Adult Book of the Year, as well as two juvenile novels, *The Half-Pipe Kidd* and *Thunder Ice,* a finalist for the Geoffrey Bilson Award, and the Manitoba and Red Cedar (BC) young readers' choice awards. She has also published a picture book, *Grandpa's Music – A Story About Alzheimer's* (Albert Whitman & Company).

Alison Acheson has taught in the creative writing program at the University of British Columbia, and continues to teach and write in the town of Ladner, British Columbia, where she lives with her spouse and three sons.

*Check out www.alisonacheson.com.*

Printed and bound in Canada by Transcontinental Metrolitho.